THE
BELLY
OF THE
WOLF

THE
BELLY
OF THE
WOLF

R. A. MacAvoy

WILLIAM MORROW AND COMPANY, INC.
NEW YORK

It is the policy of William Morrow and Company, Inc., and its imprints and affiliates, recognizing the importance of preserving what has been written, to print the books we publish on acid-free paper, and we exert our best efforts to that end.

Library of Congress Cataloging-in-Publication Data

MacAvoy, R. A.
    The belly of the wolf: volume III in the Lens of the World series / R. A. MacAvoy.
        p.   cm.
    ISBN 0-688-09601-8
    I. Title.
PS3563.A25316B45   1994
813'.54—dc20   93-22924
                                                                CIP

Printed in the United States of America

First Edition

1 2 3 4 5 6 7 8 9 10

THE
BELLY
OF THE
WOLF

At that time we were living in Canton, my daughter and I, in what is said to be the largest port in the world. The Cantoners justify this claim by equating the Harbor with the entire country. Considering the shape of the land and water (mostly water) that makes up Canton, I will give them no argument. We were residing at the medical college, where I was translating manuscripts and she was pretending not to teach, when I read in a newspaper that King Rudof of Velonya was dead.

I remember I was in a coffee shop, and the paper I was reading (I have good vision for my age) was not mine, but belonged to my neighbor to the left. There was some small disagreement about the possession of the paper, which in my astonishment and shock I did not notice. When I became aware of myself again, I was holding the owner of the paper with his hand locked behind his back in violation of both his rights and his dignity. I remedied both of these slights with money, for the Cantoners have a very commercial sense of honor, and I took the paper outside.

I sat on a box, I think, and I am fairly certain there was a ship unloading only a hundred feet away, across the stone paving of Wharf Promenade. There were cries in the air: sailors' or birds', I don't remember.

It was as though this news had ripped me out from the fabric of my life and set me down once more in a place of perfect quiet, perfect misery—ears ringing, sun too bright. I knew this place well since Arlin's death.

The article itself was short. It said the king had died in the capital, in his bed. In his bed, it said. I could see that bed behind my closed eyes: his father's bed and his father's before that, too narrow and short for a man of Rudof's build and habits. I had been allowed to visit him of a morning in his royal rat's nest, where half the covers were in a ball and the other half on the floor. He was a man who threw darts at the bedposts to punctuate his conversation. Whose feet poked holes in linen sheets.

My king, my fellow student, closer than brother. I felt the back of my head strike the bricks of the wall, for I was rocking in place like a child with fever. Huge man, quick and fiery, he had held my life in his hands, forfeit by law again and again, and he had let me fly free—he who could never himself be free. Words like these tumbled around my head, but they were only words, not real feeling. Not yet.

Dr. Keighl found me there, I don't know how long after. "I see I can bring you no news," he said.

I answered him. "You can tell me if it's true."

The doctor sat down beside me on the crate, all in his frock coat and gabardine trousers. Even at the time I knew it a great condescension on his part. "In over a year of running argument, Professor Nazhuret, we have not been able to agree upon the nature of truth. What now do you expect of me? I will say I have heard it from sources other than this poor sheet."

He called me "professor" because the university here had deigned to grant me an honorary degree of Master of Arts some years since. I had no say in the matter.

Knowing better, I had to ask, "Then, there is no chance . . . ?"

"There is always a chance."

I had asked for a platitude and had gotten one. "The news must be two weeks old, at least," I thought aloud, and Keighl answered, "Three, I am told. The Velonyan government concealed the death for over a day, and then the winter winds make shipping slow."

It took some moments for his words to form meaning in my brain. I heard the gulls; they were very loud. "The government concealed the death." I looked into the doctor's eyes, trying to be calm, to see clearly. "Does rumor say who killed him?"

With this, Doctor Keighl's figure seemed to open up, to gain movement and life, as though I had served up for him what was the real meat of the conversation.

"Of course, it is bandied about that the Old Velonyan faction did it."

"How? The paper gave no hint."

"Poison," said the doctor diffidently.

Poison could be a rending agony, or a mere falling asleep. Which had occurred meant a lot to me. I asked him what poison, and the question caused surprise. "I wouldn't know," he said. "But I would bet money that it was the queen's party that did it."

I sighed, thinking that Navvie must be told. I hoped she did not know already, had not heard offhandedly, as I had. "Isn't it curious," I said to the doctor, since he seemed so interested in the matter, "that it should be called the Old Velonyan Party, when the queen is not a Velonyan of any sort, old or new."

Then, with great sobriety, Doctor Keighl asked me what I planned to do in response to this atrocious deed. I glared at him in alarm. "Do! What on earth can I do, my dear doctor? Throw the government of Velonya into prison as a whole? Cut them to ribbons individually? What?"

The look of expectation on his moderate, oval Cantoner face did not fade. "I don't know. But I have heard about you. So much about you."

I was looking at my hands, which were clasped in front of me. Smaller hands than average, with skin slightly loosened by fifty-five years of life. I showed him those hands, as though they would communicate something to the man, and then I gave up on self-composure and ran off to find my daughter.

Canton is an easy town to run in, as all the streets are even and wide. There is poverty here, but not as much as elsewhere. There is aristocracy here, but it does not get in the burghers' way. Most notably, Canton is clean. Though the colors of its flag stand for water, its true banner should represent a windowbox of flowers. When its citizens curse (as they cursed me smashing through them along the streets), they did it with moderation and without originality. I passed along Provot Street, which was all warehouses, and across the Mariner's Park and the Old Mariner's Shelter, where one fellow passed a witty comment concerning the sight of a man my age pumping his short legs so energetically. (He, like me, a foreigner.)

The university has a large brick gate with no wall but only a short hedge surrounding it. Because the gate was clogged with dons in uniform, I did not attempt it but leaped the roses. Here the response was more outraged and less witty, because university instructors tend to regard their institution with the sobriety others reserve for cemeteries. I seem to be making this whole incident into a joke, and I cannot say why. By this time I was in pain enough.

The lecture halls were closed for the midday meal, so I ran on to the herb museum, where Nahvah had employment "arranging" the exhibits. In truth, her job was to take a large library of specimens, which over the years had been labeled and glassed by the methods of superstition and pure chance, and to match the correct plant to its Allec and vernacular names. Among my daughter's gifts is a power of memory.

She was not in the display hall; few students were. I found her in the less impressive but more useful drying houses on the building's flat roof. She was seated on a simple wooden chair, her hands in her lap and her feet folded under her skirts. I had not succeeded in finding her first.

"I am so sorry, Papa," she said. By her voice she had been crying. She was not crying now. "I know how you must hurt."

The smell of the fresh herbs around us was intoxicating. There was anise and coriander seed, giving a festive, sweet-biscuit note to the air, and beneath that odor something of the feeling of the forest floor in autumn. I knelt beside the chair to look at her closely. "But you, little academician. You are all right?"

Navvie's hair is black and thick and her eyelashes so profuse as to make her eyes seem smudged. Set within these ovals of darkness are eyes of a blue as pale as my own. Her glance is like clear sky glimpsed through black weather. My own mother I saw only once that I remember, and that time was in a dream of some sort. Yet Nahvah looks remarkably like that dream-image, even to her littleness.

"I am reasonably all right," she said. "But—though he was your friend, Papa, he was my own godfather. I knew him all my life."

Godfathers can be important relations, or trivial ones. Rudof took his godfatherhood very seriously. We had many arguments over the matter of gifts. Sometimes I won, but there was a closet of rich dresses at the statehouse in Velonya that Navvie wore only to visit the king. They embarrassed her. She would not have to wear them again.

I sat at her feet, my chin on my knees, slightly faint from the odor of the herbs and the exhaustion of sorrow. From this level I could see that Navvie was wearing her pistol in her waistband. Usually she stuffed it in her purse.

"He told me to call him 'uncle.' I was six years old, but already I knew that was dangerous, because the other children in the court grew jealous."

"Children were not exactly the problem, but you were right, dear. It was dangerous."

"So I never called him that when there were other people in the room, and he didn't correct me. So he must have known, too. That it wasn't a good idea. After a year or so, I pretended to forget."

"So did he," I answered her, though Rudof had never told me of this. "But he would have liked to have a daughter. Or a son that loved him."

Navvie sighed and her hand sought out the pistol's butt. "I

think he was easier to love as a godfather than he would have been as a father. So. What are we to do now?"

It was Arlin's gift to change mood so smoothly from the painful to the practical that my mind would stumble, trying to keep up. Navvie has taken on a lot of her mother's traits, now that she is grown. I still stumble to keep up.

I pointed at the pistol. "Do you think Rudof's death affects our security, girl? Down here in Canton?"

"There is no security," she replied, quoting Powl, whom she can barely remember. "Not anywhere on this earth. But I am carrying this because the new barrel is promised for today. I am to be at the smith's this afternoon."

As I stood up I slipped the pistol away from her and looked it over. "Were you planning to exchange the barrels with a shot in the chamber?"

Navvie put out her hand and I gave the thing back to her. "I'm not saying you're wrong, Navvie. If the day feels like that to you, keep the pistol loaded. My own feelings are too discorded for use."

We took our midday at one of Canton's coffee and pastry shops, which are far superior to the inns of my home, except that they serve a bad beer. Until Navvie mentioned the fact, I did not notice I had not eaten my dinner at all. I remember being amazed at this, and wondering whether somehow the waiter had changed my plate for a joke. I wrapped the pie in a clean handkerchief, and if I recall correctly, threw it out two days later when I encountered it in my coat pocket.

The day's inertia took us to the smithy afterward. Gunsmithery is another aspect in which Canton leaves the North behind.

I am old enough to have no feeling for guns. The two-man harquebus of my youth was as like to blow off the head of the wielder as that of his opponent. And also, back at Sordaling School, we were taught a gun was no weapon for an officer, let alone gentry or knight. But the rough tools of my youth bear little resemblance to Navvie's pistols.

She has had always an affinity for powder-weapons, which she got neither from Arlin nor myself. Perhaps it is her slightness and lack of reach that makes a pistol more appealing to Navvie than a sword, or brawling hand-to-hand. Perhaps the noise, speed, and violence of the things make a balance with the labor and compassion she exerts in her medical work. She herself says it is only the future catching up with us, and I try to catch up with Navvie as she studies with one gunmaker after another. Four countries' worth, so far.

The state of the craft in Canton was formidable. From J. Sninden of the Parade Wharf came the first pistols of standardized bore caliber, and the first presses that created leads that would fit them.

It was to Sninden's we went now, but what Navvie had in mind was a few steps in advance of the common pistol.

She had seen a weapon in Bologhini that could be loaded, like a fine cannon, from the rear of the barrel. This would add rapidity to the firing and make it possible for the user to see his packing directly, we were told. It did not work; in fact, the barrel-slide flew farther than the bullet and in a very different direction. Nonetheless, the idea stole my daughter's fancy, and she had been thinking about it for two years. In an attempt to prolong her life, so had I.

The workshop smelled so of burned powder that it reminded me of a battlefield, and the tragedy of the day made that association more vivid. Navvie had never seen a battlefield, though, and she had the resilience of youth, so she strode across the room with anticipation, kicking her long skirts with every step.

"Jonshen, did you do it? Is it ready?"

Jonshen Sninden is half-deaf, for obvious reasons, but like many another he could hear what he wanted to hear. He came out of the back room, his hands blackened and his leather apron brightened with shavings of steel.

"I didn't know if you'd be here, little girl," he said, and then he saw me and bowed, touching his forehead as though I were somebody. "Yes, I have a barrel to try, and it fits your daddy's slug-casket. No more than that can I say."

My "slug-casket" was simply a barrel within the barrel to direct the explosion forward and away from the opening on the top and back, so near to the shooter's (my daughter's) face. It held the powder and the wad and was topped with the pellet. It was to be made of steel, but I had no tools that would bore steel and no fire to melt steel, so the experimental type was of brass. Despite the fact that the presence of the casing meant the volume of powder and weight of shot had to be small, my own handiwork terrified me, and I was glad to see that Sninden had set up a vise to hold the butt of the pistol, and a target backed by a sandbox to receive the pellet. At my encouragement, he added bags of sand around the barrel and a string, the latter to pull the trigger at a distance. I think both Sninden and Navvie thought me a spoilsport.

We stood in the doorway to the room behind, and had I my way, we would have closed the door and run the string through the keyhole.

Sninden offered the pull to Navvie, as she was instigator of this experiment, but she told him she was not attached to the moment, and I heard footsteps coming up the stairs behind us as he pulled the string.

The reverberation was sharper than I expected, and accompanied by the thunk of the lead into the target and a short screech from the tall, well-dressed man behind us. He recovered himself. "Doctor Nazhuret?"

The gunsmith and my daughter deserted me.

"Mr. Kavenen," I said, to be difficult. "The doctorate is honorary."

He had recovered himself. He sniffed around appreciatively as he crossed the room to me. "Powder. What a masculine smell. Well, need we be strangers to honor, Mister Doctor Nazhuret Kavenen?" He was very tall, and enjoyed standing close.

Feeling even more difficult now, I wanted to tell him that only the name Timet went with the name Kavenen, whereas "Nazhuret" was fitted with the suffix "aid'Nahvah: aminsanaur." I escaped making myself such a fool, for I recognized the gentleman. He was Lord Damish: aristocrat functionary of the burgher-driven Cantoner Council. I had hung over that council in the visitor's gallery, where every human being had the right to watch proceedings, and heard the seventy-six councilors in their flat, Cantoner voices debate their infinite question of tariffs. The house of Damish is like the skin of the totemic lion: powerless but kept around to flourish when real authority lacks color.

"My lord, what can I do for you?" I asked, to cut through the *politesse*. I wanted to be left alone today. I wanted to see what the explosion had done. I feared Sninden and my daughter would be carried away by enthusiasm and do it again, this time without me.

He bowed, leaning over my head. "I come to offer you the sympathies of the state, sir. In your loss."

I almost laughed at the idea of a state having sympathies. Most nations seem to have only the most selfish of emotions, and Canton had none at all, only rates and tariffs. I asked the man how he had chosen me for his condolences, and he said, "It's common knowledge you were one of King Rudof's closest friends. That you knew him from school."

"No, I didn't," I answered, and I crooked a finger for him to follow me into the dim, armored room where Sninden and Nahvah were bent over the barrel of the breechloader.

"It worked splendidly," said the gunsmith.

"We can't get the casing out now," added Navvie, who has no more courtesy than I have. "I'm working on it with a pry."

I approached the steel barrel and felt it. I put my hand on the flange of brass at the bottom of the slug-casket.

"Watch, Papa. It's still hot," she said, and I returned that I believed her. I blew down the barrel, forcefully, getting a faceful of stink and oily dirt, and I heard her say the thing was coming out.

The little casing looked sound, except for the discoloration where the primer had struck powder and the smears of brightness where it had been forced from the barrel.

Sninden was magnificent at ignoring the lordship in his gallery. "The idea is sound, girl. Only the slug-casket needs to be reduced in size a trifle."

"Then it won't block the backfire, and we'll be where we started, with blown breeches and split barrels."

The council lord plucked my sleeve and I was led again into the display room. "You subject your daughter to that stench and noise, sir?" He was ready to make a joke about it. A friendly joke.

"No, I abhor guns. She subjects me," I answered, and once

again I asked the state's man—the stately man—what he wanted of me.

Lord Damish stared at me a long moment and then asked very plainly what I was planning to do about the death of King Rudof.

I had resented the man's artificiality, but I resented more his pointed honesty. "He is dead, I'm told," I answered, "and it's too late to do anything at all about it."

Dead. "If it is dead, then it had better pass out," had said Arlin, about a miscarriage. Arlin, too, was dead. Could one word stop so much?

"Are you planning to return home?"

I told him I had no plans. That was true enough. I might have as perfectly told him that I had no home.

"I ask because Canton is concerned. Canton is concerned because Lowcanton is concerned. It's not vulgar curiosity on my part."

I shrugged. "I'm sure it is nothing vulgar, on anyone's part but, my lord, I still have no plans."

The tall lord sighed. "I obviously came too soon. Please send for me when you have thought." He stalked the length of the room and then bowed. "Duke Timet." Then he bowed again. "Aminsanaur." I heard him going down the stairs.

Navvie was at my back, as was Sninden. "Papa, you have more sets of names than anyone I know."

"He certainly put me in my place with them," I said, and Sninden dropped the cooled brass casing in my hand.

■   ■   ■

That evening the port of Canton was more beautiful than I had ever seen it. The quiet water, deep enough not to be muddied by traffic, lapped at the multitude of piers. The wavelets were bright and the piers were black, in a pattern like winter branches against the sky. The real sky was washed in flesh colors: pink, ivory, and sallow, and someone hidden was playing a reed box with tinny, lonely sounds. I sat on the upper floor balcony of our little house, halfway between grief and sulking, for there was nothing in this landscape to remind me of my dead friend and king, and it seemed unfair to have no tools for my mourning.

Lights came on in the streets below, because Canton is too busy to close down at sunset; its commerce goes daily until exhaustion.

It seemed to me I had never given Rudof half enough in recompense for all he had done for me. I remembered all the times I had paraded my refusal of the simplest duties a subject owes his king. I would not war for him; I would not accept his authority over me nor the authority he wished me to take up over others. What was it I had said to my king, on our first meeting, on the southern marches of Zaquashlon? "Let us not stop here like fools discussing my accent . . ."

Why was I still alive and free after all that? He had been known as a touchy man. A redhead.

His only surviving son was a redhead also, and the boy had never appreciated my qualities. The boy was now a man: the king of Velonya. I was not entirely unhappy to be away from Velonya as he ascended the throne.

Navvie was standing at the balcony with me. Her hands gripped the balustrade and she allowed her feet to swing between the uprights. There were green stains on her fingers and she bore a smell of crushed grass. "I don't know if the railing is safe," I said.

"It will hold my weight," she answered, with the complacency of the very small. "Or do you think I should be acting my age?"

This was so ridiculous I didn't respond. Nothing I have taught Nahvah has had anything to do with acting one's age.

"By my age," she continued dreamily, looking at the thirty-foot drop beneath her, "I am really a hopeless old spinster."

My daughter is twenty-seven, though she looks fourteen. I asked her if she even knew how to spin, with the idea she would turn a toe-pirouette on the wooden slats and then laugh, and maybe then I could laugh, too. But Navvie did not give me that laugh. She just shook her head. "No. Mother did not remember how, so she could not teach me. Unless you mean spinning a blade."

"Still, that's a form of spinning. I suppose you qualify as a spinster—and will even if you marry."

"Marriage doesn't run in my family," Navvie said calmly. "Neither my mother nor my father ever married.

"That was just a joke," she added, after staring at my face. "Please, Papa. Just a joke."

There was very little light outdoors by now, and I left the piers and the ocean for lamp-lit rooms and dinner.

I was thinking of young Jeram as much as I was Rudof that evening, wondering what effect the political turmoil would have on his troublesome little philosophy, which the boy called a religion and which he blamed on me. Ofttimes I have wanted to hang Jeram, for his enthusiasm was only matched by his ability to miss the essence of things. I did not want anyone else to hang Jeram, though. What a miserable shame it would be if he died for a teaching he didn't even understand.

Navvie opened a bottle of wine. I did not know when she had purchased this luxury; I was too depressed at the moment to ask. In retrospect I guess she had the bottle ready to celebrate the success of her breech pistol, and instead it went to help us drown the sorrow of Rudof's death.

Navvie's mother used to while away the time putting dagger holes in rented furniture. Navvie herself always leaves things in better condition than when she found them. Our souls come out of a grab bag, I think, and our parents have limited power to endow or influence. Tonight Navvie seemed to be mending and freshening clothes. I watched her, scarcely seeing.

"The church, Papa? Is that what's bothering you? Your expression is more peeved than grieved."

"Rudof has certainly peeved me as well as grieved me, child. But you're right. I am wondering whether your friend Jeram's silliness has gotten him into final trouble."

Navvie sighed at me as I often have sighed at her. Or her mother at both of us. "It isn't fair to blame Jeram on me, Zhurrie, just because we are both of an age. It's you he reveres. Besides"— she stacked three folded blouses and pounded the pile flat—"'The Belly of the Wolf'" is not entirely silly. If he hasn't understood your practice very well, you haven't spent much time teaching him."

I protested that I hadn't wanted to teach him at all. It had not seemed appropriate. "But he refused to understand that. He broadcasts his own lessons like grass seed, come stone or soil. And he did not hesitate to set himself up as a teacher before anyone complimented him on his wisdom."

Navvie finally gave me the giggle I wanted. "Oh, poor man, if he had to wait for compliments, he'd be tripping on his beard before he could start to lecture. He waited so long to be taken seriously. Especially by you."

The wine was bright and rough, probably produce of Canton itself. "I fear that the Norwess Provincial Assembly will be taking him more seriously than he'd like, from now on . . ."

". . . If the crown party leans on them," I concluded, and for a moment the wine was like blood in my throat.

"I know," said Navvie.

The last veil of numbness ripped away, and I was no longer able to pretend this death—this assassination—this murder had nothing to do with me, or with the people I touch. "We shall probably have to do something about all this," I said. I looked at Navvie through the ruddy lens of the wineglass, and I saw what she was doing.

"I know," she said again. "That's why I've been packing."

■　■　■

It was the middle of the night when I woke, out of a dream not about Rudof but concerning Arlin, who was explaining to me why she would not return with me on the wharfside horsecar. It had something to do with the weight the poor beasts could pull, I remember, and I was telling her she had grown so thin with the cough the horses wouldn't feel her. She held out an omnibus card stub, saying, "One trip is all you get for your ticket," and she walked out, ankle-deep, into the sandy water. Her intransigence made me angry, but when I woke I was not angry but wet-eyed, and there was someone moving about on the downstairs floorboards.

I had given up carrying my dowhee on the overcivilized streets of Canton, but had not lost the habit of putting it under my bed at night.

At the top of the staircase was a shape, but I knew that shape; Navvie was not the source of this midnight disturbance. From birth she moved without noise: an astonishment to her mother, her father, and their teacher as well. She also had the good ears of youth.

In Navvie's right hand was a pistol—not the experimental weapon but a serviceable thing we kept loaded in the closet of her room. In her left hand was one of her mother's beautiful, nasty throwing knives. "There are two," she murmured in my ear. "They are looking for the staircase."

Incompetent. Or perhaps the intruders had not been given time by their employers to prepare for this—what? This kidnapping, murder? I made a quiet suggestion into Navvie's ear as the first of the two found the stairs. We withdrew, she to the lavatory doorway, and I to the shadows at the end of the hall.

The men carried razors, which caught the slim light coming through the hall window. My dowhee's gray blade did not. As the second of the assassins (for so I had to call them) came tiptoeing past the head of the stairs, I struck him hard with the pommel of the dowhee and the sound rang in the air like a spoon against a wooden bowl. He grunted and died thereby, for his companion spun around in reflex with his razor out and slit half the man's face and half his throat. I think he died unconscious.

There was a good opportunity to take the other one down while he stared at the work he had done, but I did not want to kill him if I could avoid it. My dowhee had almost three times the reach of his blade, and I knew my house.

He was soaked and spattered with blood, and it ran in his eyes. Blinking, he made a screaming charge for me and I struck at the razor with my heavy blade and deflected it. Then the assassin's screaming was drowned out by a huge report and his bloodstained face was orange-lit and I heard the small but distinct splat of his shoulder joint exploding. He screamed again.

"You made it hard to get in a shot, Papa," said Navvie. Methodically, she checked the barrel for wadding, tested its temperature, and stuck the pistol into the sash of her nightrobe. I went out to find a militiaman, leaving Navvie with one drained body and a bound, wounded man with a very foul mouth.

Navvie had seen it all before, and sometimes her father felt very unhappy about this. When I said as much, she told me being a doctor was harder on the nerves than any scrape I've gotten her into. I would like to believe this.

The militiaman, as I recall, was an immigrant from Morquenie: a blond Velonyan. He charged up the staircase and was sick on the hallway carpet runner. After that, many other militiamen came, and we were made to tell our story a number of times, and our sullen prisoner was taken away. His shoulder was a ruin, because of the soft lead Navvie uses in her pistols, but it had been neatly cleaned and bound. The rug soaked in the blood of his fellow would never be usable again.

"They were agents of Lowcanton," said Navvie as we rolled the carpet up and pushed it out an upper window. "Hired in Boxan last week. They were supposed to do us in two days ago, but the weather made passage slow."

The best thing about our borrowed house was the water tank in the lavatory, which gave us water on demand both in the kitchen and upstairs. Navvie pumped for me and helped me try to remove bloodstains from my nightshirt. "He didn't say a damn thing in front of the militia," I said. "Nor in front of me, unless you count his expletives."

She smiled. The expression was softened by her youth and by candlelight, but I suspected it was the predatory smile of Navvie's mother that I was seeing. I remembered my dream again. "Of course not. Assassins rarely betray their masters. But to me it wasn't betrayal, but bragging. I didn't count. Not a . . . a little thing like me." Now there was no mistaking the quality of Navvie's smile.

"So, Papa. This answers the question of whether the king's death was murder, doesn't it?"

I dried my hands and dabbed the towel against my cold, wet shirt. "We still can't be certain about that."

She laughed. "All right. I will bet you ten tepels against your three tepels that we discover it was murder, and connected with this attempt upon us."

I told her I did not enjoy betting, and she laughed at me again. Her mother's laugh. We were out of that house before sunrise.

■ ■ ■

When I was young I had no difficulty parting with things. I had no things of my own, and it seemed the world was so cluttered with useful and curious objects that I would bang into all I needed, even if blindfolded, and that I would lose them, too. My teacher's warnings about the impermanence of things in life seemed no more than attempts to convince me that snow was white.

Now that I am past fifty, I know the pain of admitting that I can't take things into tomorrow: not that mitered glass cutter, that single-spotted puppy, that perfectly balanced knife, that book of ephemera, that shirt with double-turned seams (not too long in the sleeves, for once), that dear and closest friend, and that Nazhuret.

To be accurate, the last of these I have lost so many times I'm never sure I have him. No grief there.

The cutter, the knife, and the shirt were left behind in Canton. The puppy was left earlier—he found a home with a young lady at the Rezhmian court five years ago. The book of ephemera I still have by me, waiting its turn, but at this time Arlin was almost four years dead.

■ ■ ■

So civilized was this city that we effected our secret escape on an omnibus car, both of us carrying a dowdy bag made of carpeting and an odd-shaped canvas case filled with odd things: a survey tripod, two small telescopes, and an assortment of glass and swords. I had wanted Navvie to bring along her Cantonese collection of medical and surgical tools, but with the ruthlessness of youth she had pronounced them replaceable. I do not know now whether she noticed I had packed them all away with my clothing.

My dream of the night before came very clearly to me as the

four huge horses pulled the vehicle over the flat, flat pavements toward the university. There were no hills in Canton: no reason to get out and walk. There was no one using this route but us and our luggage; not even the dawn colors were up for the day. I had a distinct feeling of farewell toward this gray stone, the heavy blond horses, the dark and sensible driver, dressed so much better than a man of his station could dress in Velonya. I had liked the city.

Navvie and I left our luggage in a heap blocking the stone walk by the arts quadrangle. She went to find the Medical Dean while I made my excuses to the Warden of Philosophy, by whose invitation we were in the university and in Canton. He was not surprised at my leaving. He said that in the last twenty-four hours I had become unusually popular, but that he could not venture to say whether that ought to make me stay or to hurry.

Lord Damish, I thought, and said the name aloud.

"Count Sibold," the warden answered, astonishing me.

Sibold was not a count of Canton; the city-state has only vestigial nobility. He was Lowcantoner. Once he was ambassador to Velonya, and in Vestinglon I had met him and judged him dangerous. Now both he and I had come to Canton.

There was a bird singing, though it was midwinter. I went to the warden's deep window and sat on the sill. "The ambassador himself? Or do you mean one of his men?"

"I mean Sibold. He came dressed like an honest burgher instead of a count."

"I knew an earl, once," I said, still seeking the bird among the skeletal locust trees of the quad, "who dressed more like a burgher than the richest brewer ever born."

"I know," said the warden, with a hint of warmth. "I read your book."

I felt a moment's shock and leaned my forehead against the glass. "I didn't publish that history," I said, holding back a dozen sharper retorts. "A young idiot named Jeram did. Out of personal letters."

This sullenness was not fair of me. The warden had invited us to his country, paid for a great deal, and now was put into political danger with us. I started to apologize, and he started to wave it aside when another thought occurred to me and I interrupted myself.

I asked the warden when Count Sibold had been by—yesterday or today. He said yesterday, late. After the campus had begun to buzz with the news of King Rudof's death.

The warden was a large man, probably of northern heritage, like so many in the city. He came to sit next to me on the windowseat, his academic robes of red and gray spilling over the open window and down the outer bricks. (In Canton only the university doesn't dress like an honest burgher.)

"I did not tell him where you were staying," he said to me. "I told him you and your daughter had moved out of guest housings into your own establishment."

I had to grin at this spark of conspiracy, coming from a man like the Warden of Philosophy. "But it was no secret: where we lived," I said.

"True. But Canton does not tell Lowcanton. Not for free," he said. Among these honest burghers, it is more than a proverb.

■ ■ ■

Navvie was not with the luggage, so I trotted over to the school of medicine, which being practical and useful is not permitted on the university proper. There, amidst the odors of blood and opium, I walked in upon her being embraced by the dean's first assistant.

Navvie did not appear either involved in or angered by the young man's display, so I did not feel obliged to intervene or to withdraw. After a few moments, during which he poured tearful entreaty into her ear, he noticed me and sprang back.

"So," he said. "I am told that we must bid farewell. I am sorry to see your daughter go. Very sorry."

At his age, I could not have handled the situation half so well, but then, I would not likely have been embracing a girl in university chambers.

Navvie led the way out again. "Old Dean Aulen could have

been more pleasant. He took the line that the college had invested time in me and that my walking out in midterm was a sort of theft. Can you imagine? When they never even accepted me as a student, let alone a Fellow."

"What sort of line was young Fepper taking?"

My daughter groaned. "Just what you saw. Such an embarrassment! I had no idea he would do something like that." She walked out onto the sidewalk with the self-composure of a cat.

"You never *do* have," I said.

The luggage was not on the pavement where we had left it, but a passing student told me it had not been stolen—nothing is ever stolen at Canton Old University—but picked up by the grounds keepers. The only thing the honest burghers hate worse than theft is untidiness. By the time we had picked up our bags and apologized in three separate offices, all hope of leaving early or leaving unnoticed had faded. We took another omnibus to the Embarc, hoping to catch the eastern packet boat, which left every day at noon. Yestereve's bright sunset had ripened into rain.

Travel in winter on the Morquen Sea is a miserable thing, but Canton's regular service stops for no wind or wave. There is a certain basic humility in the arrogant Velonyan, engendered by the violence of his winters. The Cantoners lack arrogance, but also lack enough ice to make them humble.

This is not to say they do not get sick in their barrel-bottomed, groaning ships. More than half the passengers heading east out of port lined the rail like so many balustrades—retching balustrades. By luck neither Navvie nor I is subject to seasickness, but the atmosphere was nonetheless unpleasant. Spray wet our clothing, but belowdecks smelled too much of vomit to make us want to retreat. She worried about her black powder in the damp; I worried about our health.

The wind blew at a good angle, perhaps twenty degrees from the bow, and I sat myself there in the battering chill to clear my head.

My teacher taught me, thirty-six years previously, to sit still. In an effort to distract a babbling nineteen-year-old from his babbling, he used the old story of the black wolf of Gelley, which had nothing in its belly. For the next thirty years, I called this process of self-collection "the belly of the wolf." Arlin borrowed the phrase from me. Jeram Pagg stole it outright and stamped it over his own philosophical baggage. Now I disliked the much-abused old fairy tale and the phrase itself, which had come to stand for some sort of dark magic, some mystery with secret words and secret gates of knowledge. I am supposed to be the father of this sect and in it I am much revered. Damn them all—I have only one child, and that not a religion but a girl: Nahvah, named after her grandmother whom she never met. Navvie's daughterly reverence is minimal.

All I had left of that aspect of my history was the sitting still. It is enough of a mystery and enough of a gate for me. I sat in the hollow of a rolled-up rope, under the clean wind of the ocean, and did not think about where we were going.

The captain came by, holding to the rail. He was a Felonk; a heavy-built, russet-skinned man not much taller than I. He was not sick, I was glad to see. He recommended my moving to the center of the ship. He went away again.

Clouds tumbled in the sky. In the moments when the sun shone through, the water around us was a cold blue. Most of the time it was a frozen gray, only slightly darker than the clouds. I did not particularly look at it, but when a long neck arched above the bow of the ship, I felt my balance shifting, and I went from the belly of the wolf to the orange eyes of an improbable sea monster.

The deck rose four yards above the water, and the creature's head hung well above the rail. That head was as large as I am, and shaped somewhat like that of a draft horse, though no horse has such a pair of ears, stiff and webbed and slightly iridescent, even under the diminished sun. The gray skin, too, had an oily sheen.

The apparition rose above the rail and fell as a wave lifted the ship, and then it was back again. Its mouth was closed and it did not blink. I wanted very much to see the rest of it, and I wanted very much to be away from that spot in the hollow of the rope, within the stretch of that long, pillar-like neck. While I was still between these two impulses, the creature gravely sank into the water and did not rise again.

It was another half-hour before I went to find Navvie, and in that time the wind subsided somewhat, but I found the smell of the ship to have grown even worse. Navvie was busy treating the suffering—not with sophisticated medicine, but by the old wives' remedy of squeezing the wrists. Her tiny hands are strong, and she has always had the proper touch.

The captain was kind enough to praise her to me, and he suggested the shipping line hire her to accompany all spring voyages. He laughed as he spoke, so that I would be sure it was only a joke.

I said, "Captain, did you know there was something in the water investigating your ship a little while ago?"

"In the water? Oh, yes. He is Pilot Pol, an old friend to sailors on the Morquen. He keeps us company, and he will guide a ship through the rocks of Sevech Harbor. Once he even indicated that the tide was too low for the approach to Morquenie. That was before the dredging, of course."

I have no great experience as a sailor myself, though I have been passenger on a number of long voyages. I stared at the complacent, square face of the Felonk and wondered how I could have missed knowing about such a beast. "Pilot Pol? Well, he certainly does have the eyes of a parrot. I never heard of his kind, though."

"Why should you have heard of him? His world and yours are very different."

I agreed with the captain.

"He is a great silverside, and their home is mostly in the East, and in warmer waters. I am glad you saw him, for we missed him in port, and I feared some scoundrel had taken a shot at him again. Once before it happened, and Pol left the ship lanes for months. Nor will he ever guide that ship again—*The Worrel Provider*. I wouldn't hire on to her for my pension, for I'm sure I wouldn't live to enjoy it."

I leaned over the rail, letting spray batter my face, and I shouted back to the captain that I had heard stories like that about dolphins, from time to time.

"Well, of course he *is* a dolphin and nothing else," he answered, also shouting. "Only of a large kind, and unusually marked."

I straightened up. "Very large, Captain, and very unusual. I don't think this was a dolphin I saw. It was more like a snake."

He nodded forcefully. "They can give that impression, to a landlubber. You must not expect them to look like the statues: the carved candlesticks. In the water a dolphin looks like quicksilver with a fin." Clapping me on the shoulder, he left me with my confusion intact.

That evening the sun sank very bloody, and the water, too, sank—to a flat, twitching surface. I found salt crystals throughout my hair. Navvie was very tired and she was hungry, as was I. Had we been ravenous, we could not have made a dent in the food presented to us: good food in the usual heavy style of Velonya. No one else seemed to be eating at all.

It was either the next day or the one after that when Navvie came and told me we had Count Dinaos on the ship. Until this time my only immediate worry had been our stopover at Kast, in Canton itself. If the Cantoners were looking for us, we would then be in trouble, but as we were traveling under different names than our own, it would require real effort on the government's part to inconvenience us. Dinaos, however, might be an inconvenience at random; he had the reputation of a quarrel-breeder and a duelist. Such as he have not existed in Velonya since Rudof's father's time.

"Stay away from him," I said to Navvie. "Even at the expense of remaining belowdecks until after Kast. Don't let him know you exist."

My daughter sighed. She was polishing one of her mother's knives. "Too late, Papa. He was sick as a crow yesterday and I treated him. I didn't give him my name, either the true or the false, but he does know I exist. Besides, he is one of the finest portrait painters in the world. Why should I avoid him?"

"Because he is known to paint portraits of the men he has slain: tombstone miniatures. Avoid him."

Though I reckoned that Navvie's kindness might have softened the fellow's scrappy heart, I watched her continue to clean the weapons, one after another, and I approved. That afternoon a tall, thin fellow in brocades accosted me at my position in the coiled hawser. He cleared his throat. He did look pale, despite the flat seas.

"You, sir, do not have the face of a civilized man," he said to me as he leaned against the wheelhouse wall.

"No, sir, I do not," I answered wholeheartedly, showing no more resentment than I felt.

He walked around me. His eyes were calculating. "I request the honor to paint you."

"Alive or dead?" I answered him, rising up and turning, so he would not be entirely at my back.

He cleared his throat. He had the coldest stare I had ever seen. "By God, in motion, if I could. Why do you ask? Is there reason I would prefer you to be a corpse? Are we enemies?"

I hopped out of the coil, which was constraining me. "I certainly do not desire to be your enemy, milord. But you have been known to paint with . . . an aggressive brush, shall we say?"

He was dark and pock-faced. He came close. Though he wore a rapier, his right hand propped his chin and his left hand supported his other elbow. "I do not murder unarmed men," he said.

"I know who you are, Nazhuret, son of Velonya and Rezhmia. I had the honor to meet your beautiful daughter yesterday."

I could think of nothing to say.

"As a noble of Lowcanton, I have no reason to feel friendship, or even tolerance for you. And further—you are known as the deadliest man in the northern world, and of course I find that dubious. No one man could do the things credited to you . . ."

"Then obviously I have not done them."

"Be quiet. There is no need to placate me. Look at my hands."

I answered, "I see them. They are stained with various colors, most prominently madder and ultramarine."

His mouth smiled, slightly. "They are not the hands of a civilized man. I am a painter before I am a nobleman, or anything else at all. I want to paint you. Now. On the ship."

I felt a chill emanating from that long, elegant face. "As a clown, milord? Are you looking for a touch of comedy in the corner of some large narrative piece?"

The smile climbed higher on his face, but did not reach the eyes. "As an exotic, sir. A beautiful exotic."

I couldn't think what kind of game he was playing with me. I heard the water lap the sides of the ship. "You must be speaking of my daughter. She is beautiful, and to a Lowcantoner, exotic."

He looked past me at the ocean, just for a moment. "Yes. She is your daughter. But I have painted beautiful girls. I want to paint you."

"And then promote a duel, milord? Is this how you arrange your sport—with an appeal to your opponent's vanity?"

The smile died entirely. His eyes were onyx, and might have been without pupil. "I make no promises. I want to paint you. Most of the world would consider that an honor.

"And don't call me 'milord,' fool. You outrank me in two separate nobilities." He stalked away from me, with no regard to protecting his back. "In the morning," he said.

Navvie thought there could be no loss in giving the gentleman his way. She thought his odd request perfectly natural in a painter, and if he were bent on murdering me he would find it no easier with a palette in his hand, she said. Besides, she could hover nearby with her mother's little knives. In the end we compromised. I said I would be painted if she would deign *not* to guard me, but to stay at the other end of the ship.

That night the wind came up, and I hoped the count's malaise would recur and make the painting impossible. I walked out on the deck under scudding clouds to find the captain leaning out in a meditative manner. "Still no sign of him. Of Pol," he said. "Not since you saw him this morning. Off the north coast of Canton he is usually with us. Because of the rocks."

I leaned with him. "If the creature I saw really was Pilot Pol. I never knew a dolphin to have such a long neck."

He sighed, like the groan of ship's timbers. "It's called a rostrum, really. The weather will be fair and fresh in the morning."

"Too bad." I did not explain my remark, but stared into the sparkling, bow-broken water. "Tell me, Captain. Does Count Dinaos ride with you often?"

Abruptly the Felonk captain stood upright, his two legs braced on the deck. "Avoid that man," he said. "He is deadly."

"I know," I replied. "But your ship is very small and he does not want to be avoided."

He slapped his hand against the gunwale, in evident turmoil. "I'll put you ashore: your lovely daughter and yourself. As soon as the rocks are behind us. I'll send out a boat tomorrow evening."

"Tomorrow evening will be too late," I said. "Our appointment is for the morning."

The captain gasped: a very frightening sound.

"You can put my daughter ashore tomorrow evening, if you need to, and I would be grateful," I said, and the Felonk nodded to me, his eyes wide and black.

Within the hour the wind began to die down and there was barely a stir in the sails by morning.

Out of my ignorance, I brought a few props with me to the sitting—a glass blank, my battered journal, and the old collapsing telescope I had carried all my years with Arlin. My noble painter informed me he was not doing a burgher's portrait here, and sent me to pack them away and return again with my sword. The closest I have to a sword is my dowhee, which looks more like a hedge-blade than a dueler's weapon, but he accepted that.

He demanded I take off both jacket and shirt. We of Velonya are not raised to expose our pink skins to the world, and mine is especially "exotic," having three different shades of suntan and more scars than is comely. I was determined not to allow the man an excuse to quarrel, however, so I stood in the sea breeze barefoot and bare-chested, first freezing and then smelling my skin burn under the open sunlight.

He asked to see some of my practice forms, and the pose he chose was widespread and close to the ground, with the dowhee about to rise into a sword lock. At least, that's what I told the man it was. It is as easy to split a man from sternum to rectum from that position as to block a rapier, and either deed is easier than holding the damn position for forty minutes at a time.

He held his brush in the left hand. I found that interesting; I have always wondered what it would be like to be left-handed.

First all the ship turned out to watch, but painting is slow and the painter was surly, so soon we were alone but for the captain and (despite her promise to me) Navvie sitting on the opposite rail.

When permitted to, I straightened up and almost fell flat from stiffness. She came and threw a shirt over me. "Are you cold or hot, poor Papa?"

"Yes," I answered and shuffled over to the tall, battered-looking, and many-colored easel. He was still working: blocking in the ship and whatever was visible behind her in the water. I begged permission to look.

"Nothing to see," he growled. "But please yourself."

Actually, the man worked very fast. The under-whiting had been laid before, but the crayon work for form had all taken shape in this first pose. All the lines were suggestions of movement, rather than anatomy, but they were superlatively correct movement. Already, by the broadness of the cheekbones and the slanted eyes, I could recognize myself, though I thought he had flattered me somewhat in terms of proportion.

My mind filled with stupid remarks, which I recognized as stupid. "Did you expect to see it all done?" the count asked, still scratching away at the texture of the deck. His nails were cracked and filthy. Something about him reminded me of Arlin: the pride, the dirt, the competence. And the severe tongue.

"No," I answered. "I am surprised to see it as far along as it is." The bit about my face and the proportions I left unsaid.

"No time to be slow. Also no time for mistakes. Drink water and get back there again. This sun won't last forever."

The sun's position lasted for two more sessions, and mine would not have lasted much longer. At the end I was shaking like a sapling, and had the man desired, he could have slain me with a paintbrush.

Navvie was standing close behind him, I think not to be in position to defend her papa, but out of fascination. He was still at it, not scratching anymore, but daubing. He used a heavy brush and thick paint.

It was a thing of splendid light; it made me catch my breath. I stared at the honey-gold deck, the busy sky, the glints of brass, the syrupy shadows, and lastly at the figure that almost filled it. That figure terrified me. It nearly brought me to tears, and despite all my resolutions to behave well I heard myself say, "I wish I did look like that."

Count Dinaos shot me a look dirtier than his charcoal. "Do you have any reason to believe you know *what* you look like? *Milord?*"

This criticism might have been from my own teacher. "No. That is exactly what I cannot know. Milord. Forgive me."

"Papa is convinced he looks like a gnome," said Navvie into the man's ear, for all the world as if he were her close friend. I pulled her aside, under the guise of needing support to stand.

He made no return to her comment, but watched me getting my feet under me. "It's not easy to take a pose like that. Actually, I had no expectation you would last.

"When you are settled, Aminsanaur, you must send me your address, and I will paint you a sketch of this." He screwed the canvas into an awkward box frame that would keep dirt from the wet surface. "Oh, and I had no intention of challenging you. I really don't do that at random, whatever the gossips say."

He walked off, with a servant beside him lugging the equipment, and he left us there.

■　■　■

It is Lowcanton's misfortune that it has so few good harbors, and its great misfortune that it alienated its best to the point of revolution. After a stop to load at Kast (which is drear), we passed by mile after mile of picturesque black rocks breaking the surf into snow, and behind them rose green slopes and vineyards without towns, for commerce was strangled by lack of transport. Lowcanton has an old culture—some would say too old—and it is the last nation in the Northwest to have bound peasants as well as foreign slaves.

It also had gentry and a great number of aristocracy, but what was entirely missing from their society was Canton Harbor's specialty: the decent burgher.

"Papa—I saw something. In the water. It had a head like a horse and a neck like . . ."

"It's actually called a rostrum," I said to Navvie. "And the whole animal is called Pilot Pol. He helps ships through the rocks."

She stared at me, and at the now-empty sea. "Pilot Pol is a dolphin. This was no dolphin."

I joined her at the rail. The sun was going down again, and soon Lowcanton would be behind us, and Ighelun, which owes allegiance to Rezhmia but has a language related only to that of Sekret, would take its barren place. "I only know what I'm told. The captain said it was Pilot Pol."

She shook her head. "Amazing."

It was that night after dinner that the captain told me he had arranged our escape from the vessel. I remember I was the first passenger to leave the table, probably because most others were making up for yesterday's lost time with the victuals.

"I've prepared to drop one of the boats," he spoke into my ear as I stood on the single deck, watching a calm sea. "We can have you and your daughter on land before the man knows you have left us."

I had almost forgotten his offer of help the night before. "Do you think it is still necessary, Captain?" I asked in surprise. "The count doesn't seem to wish us any harm after all."

He shook his round Felonk head soberly. "That is not what my men say. And they have been talking to the nobleman's own servant. He means to murder you in your bed tonight."

I thought about this. "But the painting. And what about my daughter; does he plan to kill her, too?"

The captain shrugged. "So he took your likeness. Now he will take your life. As far as your daughter—I didn't hear. He has no need to bother killing a young woman, has he?"

"Yes, he has," I said with some confidence. "If he is going to assault me, he has. But he might not know that. Still . . ." I stared down at the darkening water. It was easier to see into the depths than into the motivations of men. "What's that?" I asked.

The captain also looked. "Oh, it's Pilot Pol at last. I was worried about him."

The spearhead shape of the dolphin was a good fathom under the waves, and so it was hard to make out specifics, but I knew without doubt I was not looking at the creature I had seen yesterday. This was no time to share this information with the captain, however. "If you send us to shore, we'll be in Lowcanton. The reason I came on this ship was to avoid Lowcanton."

"You are within twenty miles of the border, and close to the only navigable shoreline we will reach before midnight. And, Sir Nazhuret, if we wait until Ighelun, we will have waited too long."

I did not move from my position at the rail. "If you send us to shore, the count will know you conspired with us. He is a murderer. Does that not frighten you, Captain?"

The captain hit the wooden rail in irritation. "What do I have to be afraid of? I have eight men, and the ship is mine. If he killed me, could he sail it? Could he even row to shore? He'd be a dead man in five minutes, once my crew discovered."

The light was failing, slowly, but the wind was very gentle. "Then, Captain, why don't we just clap the man in irons now and avoid any inconvenience?"

He met my eyes only for a moment. "I have no proof. My men—they would fight for me like tigers, but in a court of law I would be abandoned." Now his pale brown eyes were stern and fixed. "I want very much to avoid murder on my own ship. You know what it means to have unlawful death on a Felonk vessel; some would demand we burn her."

"To sink my spirit. I know. But there is one thing I don't believe you know, Captain, and that is, in a duel between the count and me, it is not certain he would win."

"I agree," said the count, standing at the open doorway of the main cabin. His arms were folded over his chest, and he smiled. He was armed with a rapier. "It is not certain I would lose, either."

The captain snagged my left arm and began to haul me over the deck. "I don't want bloodshed on my ship!" he shouted.

"I'm sure you don't," said Dinaos agreeably. He stepped forward.

I released myself from the captain's grasp and pushed the man away from me. I stared at the Lowcantoner noble and could think of nothing to say.

The captain ran to the other rail, where two sets of cranes held the lifeboats, and it seemed he was planning an escape of his own, for he leaped headfirst into the first one. Out of it came sailing my own inelegant dowhee, which clattered across the boards and skidded to a stop five feet in front of me. I let it lie.

"You were in my cabin, Captain? You loaded our belongings?"

Dinaos, from his central vantage point, could see over the gunwale of the boat. "If so, Aminsanaur, you and your lovely daughter have very few belongings." Casually he strolled over and peered over the rocking edge of the lifeboat. "Two canvas bags, a long roll, and what looks like a telescope. How interesting: a telescope."

He stood between me and the boat. The captain, pressed warily against the bow of the lifeboat, drew a flageolet and blew on it. I heard hurrying footsteps.

Now the count drew his rapier and I picked up my dowhee. I had not fought many left-handed duelists, for there are not so many. I wondered if that was part of his strength as a swordsman.

There appeared from the stern four men, three of them barefoot Felonks. Two had clubs in their hands, but one carried the islanders' famous sling and one held a small throwing net. They approached together, like beaters on a hunt.

A sword of any kind outreaches a club, but is no defense against lead shot from a sling. Most swords, such as the rapier, are worse than useless against a netsman, but not the broad-bladed, handy dowhee. A Felonk weapon after all. I watched them come and I watched Dinaos.

"You don't really have any friends here," he said lightly, and he cut the air in a pattern that made the attackers pause.

"I know," I answered and moved toward the netsman.

"*Kwaff a rudet-el!*" shouted the captain from his perch in the rocking boat. Translated from the Felonk, that means "Kill the blond."

The net whirled at my face, but I hit the deck, skidding forward, and cut it out of the sailor's hands. He screamed; my cut wasn't clean. I heard a thud as a round of shot hit someone—Dinaos—and I heard the captain scrambling out of the boat.

A wooden truncheon was descending toward my head. It rang against my blade, and then I cut the throat of the man who held it, dousing myself in sickening blood. I heard an explosion, and a second later a weak scream, full of breath and quickly over. I pulled my feet under me on the slippery red deck.

The captain had a hole in his forehead. It was very neat and without powder. The back of his head was less neat. He lay spread on the deck almost behind Dinaos. Also on the deck was another dowhee: one I had never seen before.

The count was braced as well as could be against the side of the lifeboat. His right arm was flat against his body and he was working his hand tentatively. The rapier in his left hand had a slight tinge of red along its length, and the sailor gasping on the deck before him had a small red hole in his chest. The man whose hands I had sliced knelt in his own blood and cried, while another lay on his stomach with the jeweled hilt of a little dagger just below and to the right of the junction of neck and shoulders. There was no blood to be seen around it.

Navvie came up to us on tiptoe, feeling the barrel of her pistol for heat. She looked at the weeping sailor, and then at the one she had killed. "I was off in aim, here, Papa. The pistol makes me overconfident, and . . ." She glanced at the gory deck like a housewife in dismay. ". . . Enemies rarely come singly."

Count Dinaos wiped his rapier on the shirt of his dead man and with awkward care, put it into its scabbard. "I am in your debt, my lady. I have never been in such debt to a woman before."

Navvie sighed and produced from her bag her little powder funnel. In the same calm manner in which she mixed tinctures for medical use, she filled the gun with powder, wadding, and shot.

"Don't worry about it," she said. She took the arms of the man with sliced hands and looked at the injuries. "Clean," she said. The rapier-impaled man she looked at, but said nothing. Neither did she try to move him. She hopped over the body of the one she had killed, pulled out her mother's dagger, and with no modesty, took the count's right hand in hers and started an examination. She had difficulty, being less than his shoulder in height, and she pulled him down by the other shoulder. He met my gaze in astonishment, and then he laughed. It was an uncertain laugh.

"I don't think we have time for this, Navvie," I said. "There are other crewmen here—at least four of them, and then the passengers. I don't know what they'll think."

Dinaos slipped his right hand into his belt and drew swagger over him like a cloak. "By God, my reputation is foul enough already, my duke, my lady. All will believe I slaughtered these men as a postprandial."

Navvie leaped up and looked into the lifeboat. "Are we going somewhere, Papa? You should tell me things."

Now the rest of the crew began appearing, and one Cantoner burgher—a silk trader, if memory serves me—appeared from the cabin, stared, and vanished again. The crewmen did not seem disposed to violence, but hugged the outer wall of the main cabin, mouths open.

"How so, when nobody tells me anything? But whether or not I planned this flight, I think we'd better take it, or spend the next few days where we stand, like aurochs in a circle, waiting to be attacked by wolves."

"Another reason for leaving," added the count. "We've killed the captain and half the crew. Who is going to manage the ship? Are you nautical? I am not."

I shook my head.

"I can only handle a small sailboat," said Navvie. "More than ten square feet of sail and I'm lost."

Count Dinaos laughed once more, as though my daughter had made a joke. He laughed very often when Navvie was being serious.

"So, my new friends. I suggest we take this boat and go, as the so-kind captain intended for you to do. Only perhaps we should not sail into the most convenient harbor, eh?"

"You think he has an ambush waiting?" I asked, and at the same time Navvie said, "But what about the other passengers?"

"I think that was his intention from the beginning, my duke. These Felonka despise us, Lowcanton and High Velonya alike. They take money from one to kill the other with the practicality of a Harborman and no more scruples. And lady, I say to hell with the other passengers on this ill-disposed tub. At any moment one of them may try to kill us."

"You don't know that," said Navvie, frowning.

I could see no good end to this discussion, so I held up my hand portentously and the gesture did what no amount of argument could have done. In silence I approached a terrified sailor, who was still pressed against the wall of the main cabin. "Fellow, are you well disposed to my companions and I?" I asked him, and he nodded fit to loosen his head from his neck.

I continued. "Have you any skill for sailing this ship?" and his affirmative reply was equally vehement. "Will you be able to see her to shore without the presence of the captain?"

Navvie stepped forward and crossed her arms over her bosom, regarding the little Felonk, hardly larger than she. "Are you a rich man?" she asked him, and added, "Have you palaces in every port? Do the ears of kings wait for your pronouncement?"

Still the sailor nodded. "Make what you will of that," she said to me. "I'd be surprised if he speaks any Cantoner or Velonyie at all."

The count had his servant by the arm and whispered to him for a few seconds before releasing him. "What matter, my lady, whether any of these can sail, when none of us can do better? Do they need our company in their difficulty?"

My little daughter set her chin in a manner that only I knew. "No, my lord. Not our company, but our lifeboat. If we take one, there will not be enough room on the other in case they wreck. We will be guilty of murder: many murders."

Count Dinaos had pale brown eyes, which were flickering from

Navvie's face to my own in meditative fashion. His hand, not tense in any way, rested near the hilt of his sword. "And yet, pretty thing, I want to take the boat. How do you propose to stop me?"

Navvie was twelve feet away from the count, and that by no accident. "With this," she said, and aimed her pistol at him. At his crotch, to be exact.

Dinaos surprised me utterly by smiling. "You would kill one man who has stood your friend, to save others you do not know from a danger that may not even exist?"

"I don't have to kill you," she said, and the barrel of the pistol moved almost imperceptibly. "You are already injured, and an extra laceration in the foot or knee will be sufficient."

I saw the figure of the count's servant pattering up behind her, and moved to intercept him, but the man took one glance at the situation and swung wide. He was burdened with a set of good leather bags, which he dropped beside his master before retreating to the rail, where he stood and watched.

"This situation is piquant, but all in all, academic," said Dinaos, and he bent to open the largest of the bags. Within I saw beautiful linen and lace: nothing with paint stains. "There is a perfectly good ship's captain on board, and he will doubtless take control before he allows any harm to befall. Sieben, here, was captain of a crew of twenty-three before they caught him—weren't you, my pet?"

The servant looked up at us without expression.

"Show them your arm, Sieben."

The servant took off his leather jacket, and burned onto his upper arm was the split diagonal cross that indicated a man condemned to slavery. Most such pulled the oars for Lowcanton's heavy oreships.

"Sieben was a pirate," said the count, and in his voice was the pride of a man who brags that his dog—his smiling, fawning hound—is part wolf.

"You can handle this ship?" Navvie raised her voice to reach the servant—the slave—standing against the rail, just as I had asked the master. "You will leave him among this bunch?"

Again Dinaos said, "Sieben was a pirate," and this time he sounded even more like the man claiming his dog was a wolf. The former pirate himself nodded at Navvie's question, but in a more controlled manner than had the Felonk sailor. The wind was coming up, and he donned his jacket again.

"What if the others don't obey you?" asked Navvie, but she was reassured enough to put the pistol up. I moved between her and the count, in case her persistence irritated him unduly.

Sieben glanced at his master, and there was human feeling in his face as their eyes met. "Sieben cannot speak, my lady. He has no tongue. But nonetheless he has no difficulty obtaining obedience aboard a ship. Ability will out. And—he has a certain reputation. Now. Can we make our escape?"

I was not sure this was a good idea. I was not sure of anything. We might have stayed till morning and made sure the land we struck was Ighelun, but we might not see the morning. The ship's crew and passengers had begun to crawl out of the cabin, and there was no reading those wary faces.

Dinaos's bags were dumped into the lifeboat, but he called a halt to everything and sat upon one of the boat's crossplanks and began to compose a letter. When he was done, he called for a flaming wood splint, melted wax, and sealed the thing with his carnelian signet. The slave took it, blew the seal hard, and thrust the sheet of paper under his shirt.

"It says he is acting for me. Otherwise, a man with the brand will lose his life for taking such authority."

I knew this much, but Navvie had not grown up in the presence of slaves. She looked at the roughly dressed Sieben with a girls' sympathy. "Should I leave him a pistol, Papa?" she asked.

Count Dinaos made great circles out of his eyes. "Your pistol, my lady? What a sacrifice. With what will you protect yourself against me if you give him such a gift?"

She sat by the midoars of the boat, her legs curled under her. "Well, my lord, you might find out."

I asked both of them to stop this bickering. Navvie sighed, Dinaos stared, and the boat began to descend, winched down by the invaluable pirate. "Don't you lose my oil study, Sieben," shouted Dinaos. "And if it dries dusty, I will bury you in cinders!"

Sieben grinned back at the count, as though something very different had been said. I wondered at the empty cavern of the mouth behind those broken teeth, and I wondered what sort of loyalty a broken pirate might have.

The water seemed much rougher in a small clinker-built row-boat. I took a set of oars and Dinaos approached the other, to be immediately replaced by Navvie as his wound and the movement of the sea did their work on him.

The tall side of the ship receded very slowly, more from its own forward motion than that of our little craft. It seemed Sieben's first act as captain was to throw the bodies of the slain into the water, where they floated around us. I wished he could have waited.

The light was low, but there was a moon just two days short of full, and by its light I could see the white glow of beach beyond the waves. Also the black of rocks. I wondered how much control we would have of the boat once it was pulled by the surf. I am an inelegant swimmer, and Navvie has had little opportunity to practice.

The Lowcantoner was curled over the bow, sick once more and making noises. It did not seem appropriate or kindly to ask him if he could swim.

We were making progress, for the shore was closer, but I doubted it was our work that moved the boat, for the bodies had kept good pace with us. The dead Felonk captain lay bobbing off to port, face up, blandly looking past the sky. I shoved the body with an oar, but it only sank and rose again, and I settled back to rowing.

I heard Dinaos make a sound not like that of emesis, and I glanced up to see him pointing into the dark water.

"That's it," said Navvie in wonderment. "That's the thing I saw. Only it looks a lot bigger from down here."

I shipped my oars and scrabbled for the dowhee, though I had small faith in its usefulness against the horse-headed creature that swam toward us, towering above the waves.

Once again Count Dinaos laughed, as he had at the threat of

Navvie's pistol. "What a trip we are having," he cried, half-standing in the rocking boat.

Close up I could see the creature was not scaled, like a fish, but had a pebbly skin, a limp frill around its neck, and many, many little teeth. Navvie had her pistol out again, and into her ear I whispered, "Only if it shows aggression. It may be the shot will only anger it, and why take the chance?"

Through clenched teeth she answered, "I will do more than anger it if I hit it through the eye and into the brain. But it will have to come closer."

Dinaos had crawled close to us. "Closer? Perish the thought! Goddess of the hunt you may be, my lady, but let's . . ."

He got no further when the creature struck, with great speed and a lot of spray. Its target was neither us nor the boat itself, but the body of the dead Felonk captain, which sank under the water and did not rise again. All three of us stared into the black water as though patience would allow us to see into the darkness. After five minutes the water swirled farther out, and the sailor Navvie had stabbed simply vanished.

"This is becoming boring," said Dinaos, though his voice betrayed no boredom. "Let's continue toward shore." All sign of seasickness was gone from him.

Soon the direction of the water seemed to change and the waves became more linear. "Approaching surf," called Navvie. "How much surf I don't know."

I didn't like the feel of this, but as I had no alternative to offer, I just kept rowing. Then my daughter added, "Here he comes again, very close to the boat this time."

We waited for the impact. "No. It's not the monster. Look."

I paused and leaned out to see the shape of the big dolphin, Pilot Pol, almost as long as the lifeboat and almost as frightening as the horse-headed creature. It blew its breath beside us and Dinaos held his nose. Again he pointed, this time at the dolphin's smooth black back. "Look at the wounds. Look!"

There were more than a dozen red weals running diagonally across the animal, right behind the blowhole. Its handsome dorsal fin was torn. It upped-tail and disappeared beneath our little craft, appearing immediately on the starboard side, where it blew again and raised a splash with its flukes. Hopping the water, it bounced twenty yards off at about two o'clock in direction, and slapped again.

We were bouncing, too. There was more than a little bit of surf ahead, where the white beach gleamed under moonlight. "It's playing with us," said Navvie uncertainly. "It's friendly."

The dolphin blew again and breached water completely. It gave another slap. "Follow it," I shouted, over the water's increasing grumble. "It's too sore a thing for play. Follow the pilot, by your lives!"

I could hear my shoulder joints popping with the effort I put into rowing that boat sideways to the direction of the surf. The boat rocked dizzily and shipped water with every wave, but necessity overcame Dinaos's seasickness. He bailed, using his own velvet hat.

The dolphin's tail shone white as it slipped between two crags of rock. I did not stop to wonder if we could manage the squeeze or the current; I merely set the tiller and rowed. We bashed the portside rock fiercely, staving the top two boards, but once through, we found ourselves in a smooth channel, inside a wall of ragged black stone and smashing spray. I set the bow toward the strip of white and pulled for all I was worth.

"Papa," said Navvie very gravely. "Take a glance to port."

There lay our original course, where the going had looked smoothest and most flat. The breaking surf rose up in height at least the length of this boat, and curled in a long tube, through which I could see the first stars. "It would have been ironic to die that way, and not by steel," murmured Dinaos. He was shivering in his velvets, despite the work.

"I don't see our pilot anymore," said Navvie. "But I see something down there. Maybe the sand of the bottom."

Dinaos wiped his wet face with the inside of one wet elbow. "Why, I ask you? It is a fish—we are no kin to it. Why?"

"I don't know," I answered, and then the boat ground against the bottom.

It was a pebbly beach, with rocks rising behind it. A sea wind reminded me that I was cold. Navvie, in her spray-drenched jacket and skirt, was shivering, and wounded Dinaos was doing worse. I leaped into cold water, waist-deep, pulled the boat up the incline as far as I could—which was a matter of a few feet—and I climbed aboard again to toss out our belongings. "I regret having to tell you this, but we cannot stop to rest here. The cold will set in our bones, and spread in your injury, my lord. We have to keep moving until we find shelter from the weather."

Navvie sneezed, just once, and she tried her best to quench the sound with her hands. Count Dinaos spoke through chattering teeth. "No difficulty, my lord duke. We are within a few miles of my border estate—not the most elegant of my properties, but good for a fire and a change of apparel."

By now there was so little light the beach was a strip of pale glimmer that seemed to float above a horizon of rock. Very few stars shone through the thick, gray sky. "How do you know where we are?" I asked him, though my heart was more interested in the term "border estate." Upon which side of the border were we? I had hoped strongly that Lowcanton had been left behind before we left the ship. "It's very dark out here."

"I grew up launching my own little rowboats from this shore-line. Though not, I admit, from this malicious beach here." He swayed as he stood, and when I took his hand, it was like ice.

He did not resist my touch. He looked at me, his expression hidden in darkness. His knees began to buckle.

"Leave me here," he stuttered. "Take my ring. Send men back for me. I can't walk."

Instead I scooped him up in my arms. He was an awkward burden, being so long in the limb, but not very heavy: no heavier than Arlin had been. He shivered so that the silver of his belt and buttons made a bright clatter.

Navvie was prying at his sleeve as she walked by my side. "The rowing opened his wound further. He's still losing blood." She then disappeared for some moments, leaving me to find the path into the black hills. I was not worried about my daughter; her movements are as quick as a songbird's and as unpredictable. Before I had hauled my burden past the sound of the surf she had returned, her hands filled with something furry, and her pack bouncing on her back.

"Dried sea moss, Papa. It's good for packing wounds like his. Cleanly."

I stopped and leaned against a rock while Navvie ripped open the brocade of Dinaos's vest and the linen of his blood-blackened shirt. With more firmness than I would have dared, she packed the soft matter against the man's skin and wrapped it there with the ruined linen. Dinaos thrashed and cried out. His words were "Mongrel bastard! Stinking mongrel bastard!" During the next ten minutes, as I scrambled and climbed, he repeated this phrase three times more, always when I joggled him, or slipped, or came up against an obstacle in the dark.

"Don't be hurt by his abuse, Papa," Navvie whispered into my ear. "I don't think he's entirely responsible."

"I know he's not," I said. He was steaming like a kettle in my arms. I even had hopes he was not referring to me at all.

We left the black rocks behind and came to fields of infant grain, reflecting the poor light in waves of silver. There was a road beneath our feet, parallel to the seacoast, and to the right of it, another road lay broad and well maintained, heading south and away from the water.

"But for him," said Navvie softly, "we could make an easy jog to the border of Ighelun; dry our clothes with mild exercise, and sleep in safety."

I sighed, for the weight of my burden was pulling at my shoulder joints. "We don't know Ighelun is safe, my dear. Only that it is not Lowcanton. But there is no reason you can't have your jog, and your night's sleep. It doesn't need two of us to take a sick man home."

Navvie put her arm around my waist, or tried to. "True, Papa, but if one of us stays, shouldn't that one be the doctor? As soon as we come to a reasonable-looking doorway, you can put him down and leave me to wake the occupants. I'll meet you along the sea road tomorrow, or whenever he's out of danger."

Nahvah had succeeded in offending me. "That's bullshit! This is the land where women can own neither business nor land, and where women without family are property of the state. Do you think I would leave you here for five minutes alone . . ."

"It looks like we go together," she said.

We went on for only two miles, I reckon, but because of the cold, the burden, and the worry, it seemed half the night. We first encountered a few hay sheds: buildings scarcely more than a thatched roof on pillars, now almost empty of last year's harvest. Next we came to huts that looked like miniature versions of the sheds, except that rocks had been piled roughly to reach to the eaves and a wooden door shoved into place in the center. Though we knocked loudly, no one came to help.

Dinaos was now groaning constantly, and the air was too cold for a sick man, however fevered. Over the flagstones of the good road I began a lumbering run toward what looked like the candles of a village.

It was a town of very old style, with tiny houses of mud and wood palings leaning for support against the stone outer wall of a castle. I knocked at a couple of houses that had lights in the upper windows, only to see the lights blown out.

Navvie's gaze was caught by the big spiked door that marked the end of the road from the sea, the door that led through the castle wall. Upon it was graved and painted a sigil, and she held up the limp hand of Count Dinaos. She has inherited my sharp vision.

"Look, Papa. We're there." Immediately she began to pound on the huge and heavy door. It made no noise. She shouted, in Cantoner. I joined her, though by now I had little hope.

There was a bawling reply, and then a loud curse, and from the west down the street came a big, heavy man, somewhat pear-shaped. When he came close, the embroidered emblem on his tall cap could be seen to be a variation upon that of Dinaos.

He was waving a bludgeon as he came. He showed no signs of stopping as he got closer. "We have a wounded man" called Navvie.

"You'll have three dead men in a minute, you goat-fucking Harborman thieves!" he roared back, and he swung at the closest thing to him, which was the head of the count.

I did not let the blow find its target, and my daughter did not permit the fellow to have another shot. With her little knife she stabbed between the bones of his hand, locking it to the wood of the bludgeon. Next she pulled hand and bludgeon up behind his back, and as he stood there wobbling with his legs braced, she grabbed his genitals from behind and sent him to the ground.

"Think of it as a favor," I said to the man, as calmly as I could. "Had you succeeded in hitting his lordship, I think he would have killed not only you, but your entire family. Am I right?"

The sheriff's man (for so I learned he was) fixed his pain-widened eyes at the face of Dinaos. He gasped and prayed to God the Father, which is the only divine aspect recognized by the orthodox Lowcantoner. He scrambled to his feet, regardless of the damage done his privates, and so terrified was he that he tried to fish the gate keys from his pocket with a hand still impaled by Navvie's jeweled knife. She removed the impediment.

The white stone of the gateway darkened in speckles, for the guard's hand was still splashing blood. As we stepped through into darkness, I could smell it, and could smell pine resin as well. Homesickness for my black Velonyan forests nearly made me reel, or perhaps it was the awkward weight of the man I carried.

Navvie led me over a walkway of gravel and stone. I hated to trust the whole job of protection to my little daughter, but I could not give her the nobleman to carry. Even if she could have managed the weight, his red heels and ringed fingers would have dragged in the gravel.

Another wall approached, this one mottled with vines instead of blood. I heard the resounding knock, and felt warmth as the air within met my wet clothes and salty face. Here was the source of the pine incense.

There was speech, very quick and in dialect, so that I could not understand, but I stepped forward so the door could not be shut on us. Beside me glimmered the face of a woman, decently dressed and of middle years, with her black hair braided and lacquered tight to her head. She did not seek out the count's face, but instead his

left hand, with the signet of carnelian. She started an almost noise-
less howling.

"We need a bed!" shouted Navvie in her seacoast Cantoner,
taking the woman by both shoulders. "And blankets! I am a doctor,
and will need water for my medicines!"

I sighed and shifted the weight. "Bellowing doesn't make the
foreigner understand better, Nahvah. And remember, it's we who
are the foreigners."

I tried in Cantoner myself, and when the lady paid no more
attention than before, I tried Velonyie, and then Rayzhia and Zaquashlon. To my wonderment, the Zaquashlon worked. Her la-
ment, if such it was, faded into a series of gasps, and she met my
gaze like a human being. I repeated Navvie's list of requirements.

The woman touched his limp hand again, with one hesitant
finger. "But he's dead. Only the slaves of the household have the
right to lay out a Conjon. You may not touch him!"

"The man is not dead; he's hot as a furnace. Since when do the
dead run a fever?"

This time she touched his lean and briny face. "Not dead?"
She did not sound much happier.

"I have an idea," whispered Navvie. She took the count's
hand from the woman's grasp, held out the signet, and pointed with
it. "A bed, you old hag! Clean sheets and hot water! Show respect
for your master or I will have your hand off at the elbow!"

In four seconds the woman had disappeared the way she had
come. I gaped at my daughter. "I do hope you've done more than
just to scare her off, my dear," I said, and Nahvah merely shrugged.

"Or impel her to have us spitted," I added.

We continued our progress along the stone passageway toward
light and the odor of pine. I heard light feet pattering nearer and
soon we were surrounded by servants, both male and female. None
of them volunteered to take the burden from me, and indeed no
one touched Count Dinaos or helped his body avoid the furniture
except Navvie and myself.

There were stairs, I remember, and large rooms with tiled
floors that echoed in an empty fashion. Navvie mentioned the

place seemed old to her: old and in poor repair. The bed to which they led us, however, was elegant after its fashion. It was a cabinet-bed, made of some black and oily wood that had been carved into an approximation of lace. The sheets were silk, but thin with age, and my practical daughter shook out one of our own woolen blankets and lay the count's filthy form upon it.

Instead of hot water from the kitchen, we were given a tripod charcoal burner and a heavy cauldron of iron. I stripped the wet finery from our patient, while Nahvah communicated the idea of towels to the householders. We had him clean, if not comfortable, and under blankets ten minutes later. Soon the air stank of angelica and other herbs.

I do not have the art of making unconscious people obey me, but Nahvah does. Though he seemed no more alive than a doll—a hot doll—he took medicine from her and he swallowed for her and even tried to roll over on command to be washed.

Imagine: the spadassassin Count Dinaos of Lowcanton, feared by the entire populace of Canton and parts of Velonya and Rezh-mia, rolling over on command. In the exigencies of the moment I put that memory away in my head, to wonder over at leisure. It took both of us to hold his hot shivering body still for the rag and towel.

The blade that hit him had come close to the lung, but by his breathing and the lack of blood in his mouth, Nahvah guessed it had not pierced the lung sac itself. Even the outer membrane, she said, would be bound to become infected if touched by steel or lead, and we could only hope. She packed the hole with a drawing poultice, and as I held up his torso for the job, I could see evidence that he had paid dues for his skill with the rapier; there were three or four puckered scars, one very near his throat, and a number of long pink seams that I doubt came from encounters with berry bushes.

"Well, it is no mistaken identity," I said to her. "This must be the wicked swordsman we were warned about."

"I didn't doubt it for a minute," she answered dryly. Then he was clean, dosed, wrapped, and warm, and there was nothing to do but watch.

Nahvah took the cauldron off the brazier and used it to warm herself. She looked around the room and up toward the rough beams of the ceiling. "This is like the old castle in Vestinglon—the abandoned one with the big stones and no glass in the windows."

"But I wouldn't pay a crown-eighth to tour it," I replied. We were both still damp, and the wool of my trousers steamed visibly up into the darkness. "This is theater," I said. "We need a witch."

"I'll do," said my daughter, and she made a circuit of the walls. Her skirt crackled as she moved: I suppose from the salt. "You know, Papa, I see previous working on some of these stones. Could it be that there was an even older building here, in the middle of nothing?"

"Lowcanton claims to be the most ancient of northern cultures. No, actually it claims to be the only culture among us. But why rebuild on such a barren site? Well, Navvie, it could be there was good harborage here once, and the sea eddies changed. Or it could be this was fertile soil, but they overgrazed it with goats and sheep. Or it could be . . ."

"It could be they are coming to get us soon. There's always that to think about."

She had reached the hangings of the window, and gave them a resounding whack in housewifely style. From my position at the brazier I could smell the mildew. I was sorry my daughter's mind was hunting that trail; I had tried to conceal from her my own worry. "You mean the guard you wounded?"

She shrugged and leaned into the window embrasure. Her small feet left the ground before she could touch the window itself. "At least there is glass here: not calves' intestines or paper. And it opens, I think.

"I mean anyone of the household or of the village who saw us. And remember, there was some surprise the boat's captain had for us. He wanted us on land close by here."

I wasn't certain of that. "Perhaps he meant the surf to do for us. More likely, we were never intended to survive once he had us in the boat."

Navvie had disappeared behind the drapery. I heard a scrape of iron, and her fist pounding the framework of the window. A gust of cold air made the glow of the brazier dance through the room, like light on water. "I don't know, Papa. I don't know what the Felonk meant, and I don't know what the Lowcanton lord means—if he lives to mean anything. I have my suspicions, but I have never felt in so ambiguous a position before."

The gust stopped. "Be comforted, daughter," I called out to her. "I have. I have."

I went out into the hallway to find what had become of the occupants of the castle who had shown us in, if not welcomed us. The chamber door had a bar, and I requested my daughter to close it behind me, and hoped she could hear me knock behind the archaic thickness of the oak. The hall was without light, and only the echoes of my footsteps and the unnamed sense that informs the skin of one's face helped me avoid the walls.

Years ago, before Nahvah's birth, I had been lost within a building of wicker, where sound, air, and light conspired to confuse me. Here I invoked again the skill I had learned there, retracing in darkness the steps I had taken encumbered by a man much taller than I. The wind had come up, and as it twisted through the lightless passages, it brought a ghost of the surf with it, and I had a vision of myself lost in the darkness below the water. Sucked down like the Felonk captain, into black weightiness.

Where the monsters lived.

At one intersection of ways my instinct deserted me, and I stood without an idea of how to go. Nor was I certain of the route I had come. I imagined Navvie by the glowing brazier, where the lacework of the cabinet-bed cast intricate shadows on a sick man's face, and the sound of his breathing kept her from being alone. I was not afraid for my witch-daughter, not at this moment. I wanted to hide behind her skirts.

I heard voices along one groined passageway: animated voices in Zaquashlon, accompanied by the sound of clattering metal. This comforted me enough to choose, for though the clatter might be that of blades or armor, I wanted it to be the sound of pots and pans. In another moment odor joined sound to lead me, and I came to a cavernous kitchen with a half-dozen shabby people clustered at one end of a heavy oak table, eating.

I greeted them in the Zaquashlon colloquial to Warvala. They stared. My stomach, impressed by the nearness of their dinner, greeted them in universal language.

"My daughter and I would be grateful for a ladle of that porridge," I said, and I took a hard chair without invitation.

They stared.

"We are hungry. I rowed your count to shore and then carried him all the way here."

The same woman who had met us at the door, and who sat at the head of the table now, answered, "The count himself will have to command the dinner, paistye. Then it will be more than porridge."

Their brown, blue, and hazel eyes were oblique, and they turned their heads slightly away from me.

"I'm not a lord—a paistye, a hut-crusher—woman. There is no need to use your Zaquash canniness against me. I've done backbreaking work for this household, and I will take my due." I rose from the chair feeling heavier than I had when I sat down, found myself bowls and spoons, and took them to the ample pot on the stove. One I filled for Navvie, and I put both down on the table where the servants were eating. I was so hungry I really didn't taste the porridge.

"You talk like you're Zaquash yourself," said one of the men. "What with your 'backbreaking work' and your 'dues' and all." Even the Zaquashlon people find their own sly stubbornness comical.

"I lived some years in Warvala and outside, keeping order in the inns," I told him. He nodded.

The old woman was not so easily gentled. "You didn't talk like any common man when you came in, nor did that—that girl of yours."

I caught her eye. "Madam. If you think I am a paistye after all, then how is it you dare speak of my daughter that way? To my face?" Her head sank between the protective wings of her shoulders, and she gave me a look I am more used to getting from snakes.

"Either I am a lord and you give me respect due to a lord, or I am a man among you, and you are bound to give a man aid when he is sent to your house on the duties of your house."

I heard the same man whisper, "Paistye or man, this fellow is definitely Zaquash."

I was finished with the bowl of porridge. I had thought I'd want another, but it filled my stomach uneasily, like briars and burrs.

"Now to the second matter. Your count will need care. My daughter must explain the use of the teas, and the tending of his shoulder."

The old woman spoke, and there was a kind of grim glee in her voice. "He doesn't have a body man here. There's no one who can do that at all."

"I'm not talking about fancy tailoring, woman. I'm talking about washing an injury. A sick man. Your master."

"Yes, yes, the master. So we can't touch him. Not allowed. Not until he's dead, and then we have to lay him out."

"He's not dying," I said defensively. I wasn't really certain.

"Then we can't touch him at all. We're house servants. His body servants aren't here, so no one can touch him. Against the law."

They all nodded forcefully. They had me now. "If I did touch the master, and him alive, then I'd die, by law. By law. So I won't."

The man who had spoken narrowed his narrow eyes and said, "But you, there. Paistye or man, you've touched him already. Lots. And if you're a lord after all, then it's none of our business. And if you're man like us, then you're forfeit already. So no fear.

"You touch his body. You feed him his tea. You do it," he said, with a fine sense of judgment.

"And that girl of yours," added the old woman.

■   ■   ■

Navvie ate her porridge more moderately than I had and, I hope, in less irritating company. "I wasn't sure we could leave him anyway, Papa. He is feverish, and there's a lot of work in forcing liquids into him."

In counterpoint to this, the count groaned. He opened his eyes, which were black mirrors from the poppy sedative. I took a candle and went over to see if he wanted something. He gazed up at me and sighed. "Barbarian angel," he said very clearly and closed his eyes and added, "beauty cuts like the light off a sword." Then he was asleep again.

"He's not with us at all," I said.

I noticed there was an alteration in the gloomy room. The absence of two of the velvet curtains made it even gloomier. These had not gone into the sickbed, as I first thought, but out the window.

"It is only twenty feet or so," said Navvie. "Down to rubble at the back of the castle. I made a ladder in case we must leave quickly."

I shoved open the casement and examined the thing. "What a good little housewife you are: so handy. And how neatly you broke the glass to tie it to the iron frame. I am proud of you."

Navvie stood behind, poking the charcoal of the brazier. At last she said, "I'm sorry, Papa. I'm really sorry."

I turned. "About what, my dear?"

"That you are so sad. About Rudof. The uncertainty. Abandoning hour home in Canton."

I felt my grief rising even as she named it. "It's for you I'm worried, Nahvah," I said to her. "This must be very hard for you."

She shook her dark head. "No. I'm still in my twenties, and many of these incidents are happening to me for the first time. There is a fascination in that, even when uncomfortable. For you, though . . ."

At my daughter's advice I sat down against the wall of the bed and allowed myself to feel fifty-five years old. I had needed it.

■ ■ ■

All night we kept the brazier burning, though it required stepping out to replace the fuel ourselves. No one interrupted us, and I heard almost no human sounds from within the stony habitation. Sometime around midnight I went looking for the earth closet, and found instead a convenience not much different from an antique garderobe.

Nahvah fell asleep sitting up cross-legged, her blanket hooded over her. I had seen her rest this way before, when she wanted to be ready to hear a patient, should he wake. I knew her knees would suffer for it, and her feet go all pins and needles, and yet I didn't want to wake her up to tell her to go to sleep again. As I watched her in the flickering light, I kept going a long dialogue with Arlin.

In my mind, Arlin becomes more vocal than she ever did in life, when she communicated by the quality of her silences. The silence of the grave is so overwhelming that it has drowned that language for us, so in my imagination she could only talk. Often we talk about Navvie.

I didn't know why she was still with me, at the age of twenty-seven. Twenty-seven is old for a woman to find a man and leave her parents. Always for some distressing and worthless man. Ten years previously, we had lived on tenterhooks because of our daughter's wild affections; there had been the assistant head groom at Velonyie Palace, who behaved like the worst of his own stallions, and then the third son of Duke Gorman, who was not only featherheaded but too close kin to me to be acceptable. From this boy's blond, bumptious mindlessness she recoiled into the arms of the chaplain-in-training to the king himself, who was so very respectful and serious she could have ground him for a sleeping powder.

We had not raised Navvie in a manner that made it possible for us to institute a rule of force at that late date. I don't know what imprudences she committed with any of these young or not-so-young hopefuls. I would not know how to ask. For a few years we wondered whether illegitimacy could be inheritable, and we would have been in no way surprised to have been presented with another stray branch to the family tree.

Then it all trickled away, and here was my beautiful tiny daughter, proficient and loving and unflappable, alone but for Papa.

She should have gone by now, I said to Arlin. I spoke silently, as always when speaking to ghosts.

Arlin considered a moment before answering. An animal, like

a dog, or even a lion, she answered—silently, as ever—bides with
its mama for a little while and then becomes too big and too much
bother, and it gets spanked away. There is no great pain there, and
little memory.

Nahvah never became too much bother, I said to Arlin, who
seemed to laugh. Little memory, she said again.

But (my dead lady continued) if a man takes the little lion and
raises it outside of its brute nature, the rejection does not happen.
Not unless the taming man forces it.

And so I should *drive* her away? I whispered. I was astonished
and worried at the thought.

The lion raised by man is not a lion anymore, she replied. So
what is it to do? What is the man to do?

I found I was rocking in place with my concern, and my head
went *thump* against the wooden side of the bed I leaned against. Is
our daughter then not a woman anymore? Have we done her such
a damage?

Arlin's voice grew sharper. She is not a brute human being.
We were very careful she should not be. Did I not remember Powl
leading her in the riddles of reason before her mouth could form her
words right? Remember the game "What makes what thing happen?" carried out to the ninth place, with both of them on the
ground, dirty-kneed and keen, and her finishing the proof-of-
reversal before the old philosopher? And the water clock she de-
signed out of bark tubes and kitchen gear before she was ten?

You should see her experimental pistol, I said proudly.

In some disgust Arlin said, I have seen her experimental pistol.

Our daughter outgrew most of the human race before she was
twenty. Yet she looks like a little girl-elf, and the brutes treat her
as a little girl-elf. So did Rudof, who should have known better.

Is Rudof there with you? I asked wistfully, but no other voice
except Arlin's answered me, and she would not be distracted. We
created in Nahvah a lonely, self-contained person. Well, why not?
The world is a lonely place, and he who doesn't feel that has a head
of wood. Besides: her blood is of all the aristocracy of the northern
nations; would you expect her to warm to many?

I was stung. Powl never taught you such ideas, I said to her, nor did we teach them to Nahvah. He said the only blood connected with aristocracy was the innocent blood they shed on the earth.

As always, when I got hot, the Arlin in my head stopped talking.

■ ■ ▓

"Good morning," said Dinaos, though it was not yet anything like morning. Called out of a dream, I thought it was Arlin again. I stood in confusion as he rumbled open the lacy wooden side of the bed.

Navvie was still in her place, and as I had feared, her legs didn't want to support her. Carrying my blanket as a shawl, I approached the man on the bed. I put my hand to his forehead and he didn't resist me.

"I don't know if you're still fevered, my lord," I said, "but your bed is damp with sweat. That's a good sign, I'm told."

He grinned with a tight mouth. "It's a damn chilly sign, Aminsanaur."

"We'll take care of that," I said, and I assisted my daughter to her feet.

Count Dinaos blinked at us in the puzzling light of the brazier. "Have you become my servants?"

"The only ones who seem to be operative," murmured Navvie, and as he still glanced around him I added, "We were not able to find the magic word to bring the household to life. There is a great deal of Zaquash legalism here, it seems."

He sighed. "Our common folks are of that ancient, stubborn line. I understand every nasal-mouthed peasant among them. I'll command obedience."

I had been entirely frustrated with the servants a moment ago, but this statement opened a flood of memories: "The word for nobleman is 'paistye'—hut-crusher," Powl had said, teaching me the outlawed language of Zaquashlon, with which he helped make me an outlaw. I saw again the face of a teamster lad in Warvala, so much like my own I recognized my foreign origins for the first time.

"I too am of that ancient, stubborn line," I said to the count. His eyes widened and his thin-cut mouth gave an undisguised giggle. "I am a painter," he said. "I can't deny the bones of Rezhmia when I see them." He looked like he would say more, but he lay his head down again and concluded. "But you would be utterly useless as a servant."

"I'm afraid so."

Dinaos took a few deep breaths and rose again, more slowly. "Fetch me one of these renegades. Force-march him in here, if need be. We're going to have need of them."

I nodded, dropped my blanket in a heap, and made for the door. Before I reached it I heard my daughter saying dryly, "You seem to have no difficulty making a servant of him after all."

As I closed the door behind me, Count Dinaos was laughing again.

Of course, the staff was all abed, and locating their little cupboard-sized rooms in that pile took me until first light. To add to my problem, each wooden bedroom door was fixed within by a diagonal wooden brace that rested in a joint on the floor. I was compelled to backtrack to the kitchen and beat a pot with a spoon until all in that wing of the house must have been awake. Awake, but not out of their bedrooms.

Finally, the room I had chosen for my drum tattoo emitted a scuffle of footsteps. When I decided someone was on the other side of the door, I bellowed, "Count Dinaos demands your attendance!"

I had chosen the chamber of the very woman who had let us in the night before and made my evening rancorous. It seemed she slept in her gown, with a hat over her lacquered hair. "So he's not dead," she said, voice devoid of emotion.

"No," I answered her. "He's up and about." I dropped the pot and spoon clattering to the floor and left them there. Halfway down the hall I turned again and shouted, "Check and checkmate. I win," and then I ran back to the sickroom.

■ ■ ■

The woman had been right; with the count commanding it, the kitchen would produce more than porridge. There were eggs in that breakfast, and white bread and lots of dried fruits, sweet ale, and coffee. The ale sent our wounded man back to sleep, but Navvie said that was probably a good idea. She had thought to prompt him to call for warm water and a tub, which was delivered after he had returned to sleep. I stood in the doorway lest the two young men who brought in the big urn try to take it out again before we could use it. I did not know how far the servants' legalism would stretch. With this warm water we were able to wash ourselves as well as the most objectionable of our salt-caked clothes. The soapy salt water I threw out the window.

When the lads returned for the copperware, I asked casually for the news. "You are the news, paistye," answered one of them, bowing warily to me.

"I meant something of more worldly importance. You see, we have been out of touch for some time. Are there no rumors, at least?"

Rumors are as much a part of the Zaquash tongue as nouns and verbs.

The lad considered the wet bottom of the copper tub. "Well, there's only that Velonya is at war. That's in the past week."

My head spun. "At war with whom, boy?" My voice must have betrayed agitation, for both fellows raised their brown, untrustful eyes to me and stood still, like deer caught by a dark lantern. "With whom?" I asked more moderately.

It seemed the lad had trouble with his words—unusual condition for a Zaquash man. "With Velonya, I guess." He hefted his end of the tub and his mate took the other. "That's all I know, my lord," he said and backed shuffling out of the room.

The day was windy. I remember the sound that whined through the hole my daughter had stuck into the window. I remember the banging of the window itself against its metal frame. Dinaos woke again in midmorning, very thirsty and hungry. We all had a second breakfast, after I had run and found the housekeeper.

"What do you do usually when you need assistance, my lord? Bellow?" I asked the nobleman.

He glanced up from his plate, shrugged and cursed (either at his wound or at the impertinent question), and answered, "I don't usually travel alone. Or with rogue northern dukes' sons." He glanced at Navvie, who was making bandages out of one of his monogrammed sheets. "Nor do I usually travel with my own doctor, but it seems I chose appropriately this time. If there was choice involved."

"I seem to recall our little boat ride being your idea," she said.

He sat up straighter and spun his silver charger to the flagstones, like a boy skipping stones over the pond. It added its racket to that of the wind. "If the alternative is being slaughtered, do you still call it a choice?"

"Of course," said my daughter and I, together. I added, "Many of our best choices in life are thus."

He gave me a long stare with his black-brown eyes. "Perhaps that attitude explains why you are here, sitting by a foreign bedstead, waiting for the Lowcanton government to discover you and take you."

I wondered at the intensity of his regard, and put it down to the tincture of poppy Navvie had administered. "We could not leave you last night, my lord. We will now, though, if you are awake enough to dominate the Zaquash horde you employ here."

He snorted, then winced, putting a hand to his injury. "I do not employ them, Duke Nazhuret. I own them. They were all bred here. When I have the choice—choice again—I'd rather tame a pirate. And as for leaving me, you will not be able to do that."

Very moderately Navvie said, "How will you stop us, my lord?"

"I'm not going to stop you, my lady. I'm going with you."

"Why?" I asked of him. "How?" Navvie demanded.

"In the coach. I think I left the coach here, when I was by last. Of course, in three years the straps may have perished, or the wheel-felloes dried apart, but I think the coach is our best hope. If these people of mine haven't eaten my horses. And why is it the best choice? Because you won't make it the few miles, otherwise. These border peasants kill whatever creature they have not seen before."

Laboriously, Count Dinaos crawled out of bed. "Get my trousers ready," he called over his shoulder as he walked heavily over the stone floor and out the door. "I'm going to the privy."

"I'm afraid he'll fall," I murmured to Navvie in Velonyie.

"No chance," she whispered back. "Arrogance buoys him up."

I studied his retreating figure. "Arrogance is only one herb to the recipe. There's something he is hiding, that one . . ."

"I think he fancies you, daughter."

Her stare was as fixed as the count's. "No, Papa. You misunderstand."

I explained. "I don't mean you like him; I know better. But there is something there . . ."

"Papa, you misunderstand." She added, "And I think you'd better have his trousers ready." Navvie gave me a brief hug as I started looking for them. "My old pirate," she said.

They had not eaten the horses, but neither had they fed them well. The four gray trotters should have been high-headed and round in neck and quarters, and instead they were skin stretched over barrels. The coach itself had been rained on, and at some time had served as a roosting spot for birds.

In a fury only slightly thinned by weakness, the count ordered the horses groomed and a good feed of oats for each. The servant who harnessed them sighed and sighed, and I was certain the oats in question had been destined for the castle kitchen.

Navvie eyed the elderly vehicle with some doubt. "Are the roads between here and the border sound enough for this, my lord?"

He was leaning upon both of us, dressed in clothes that still sparkled with salt. "Either they are or they aren't, my lady, and if they aren't we'll all roll on the ground."

Dinaos smiled at the idea. He opened the door of the coach, releasing an odor of dried leather and mildew. He slid in and we followed.

This was my first glimpse of the eastern border of Lowcanton. It was barren and rocky, and I wondered that the northerly winds could blow dry over here, cross the sea, and dump such benign moisture on foggy Morquenie and on Rezhmia's vineyards. The winter grass was dead, not from cold but drought, and the soil made an inadequate covering on the bones of the earth.

Those bones made our progress troublesome, intruding themselves at odd places in the packed road. The leather straps that suspended the body of the coach creaked and groaned every time a wheel hit one of these rocky outcrops and the seats bounced as though we were being tossed in a blanket.

The count groaned with the leather. "Ow, I would fire that coachman, if I could!" He held his injured shoulder still with the opposite hand.

"You could always free him," suggested Navvie as she supported him from the other side.

"Free him as a reward for his uselessness?" He laughed heartily, despite the pain. "Actually, dear lady, I can't. By law."

"Their laws here are very complex," I called across Dinaos's back. "I'm beginning to understand that," she returned.

The road lifted out of our bowl of rocks and emptied onto a windy plateau where a highway ran east and west. Dinaos gave a satisfied sigh. "You will not understand us while you think of us as the southmost part of your northern group of nations. Instead, Lowcanton is the northernmost of the southern countries. Culturally we are most like Claiden Range."

"But with fewer camels," I said, and he nodded.

"And monkeys," added Navvie, and after a moment the count answered. "Oh, we have monkeys, my lady. We just left a number of them behind."

My laughter died as I remembered Powl's words. "It is a provincial, narrow-minded attitude to see another group of people looking more like animals than our own race." Besides: Was it really another group the Lowcantoner was mocking, or my own? I stared out the open window at a yellow-dun world.

"You know what is the best thing about this region?" Dinaos asked, five minutes later.

"The solitude?"

"The light. Dry eastern Lowcanton by the water has the most useful light in the world."

Navvie cleared her throat. "Is one sort of light more useful than another? Assuming there's enough . . ."

"For a painter, it is. This hard, empty light is perfect. It does not interfere with the subject, but glorifies it. Except for that reason, I would never come to this dingy place at all.

"That, and the fact that I cannot sell my border properties under crown law."

We passed a colorless sort of village, where gray board-sided huts and grayer stone cottages endured the wind's blast, and rows of split fish, drying like laundry on lines, flanked the road. I saw only one person—a shape that darted behind one of the huts and did not reappear. The predatory peasants of the region had no courage before the sight of a noble's coach, however dreary and inadequately pulled.

"How far are we?" Navvie asked. "From the border?"

"About halfway," he answered, and above his voice and the creak of the coach and the slap of the trotting hooves I heard other sounds: other voices, other hooves.

Without speaking, I sought my pack on the floorboards and loosened the dowhee. Navvie leaned out the other window. "Could we have been reported already, less than a day off the ship?"

"Just," said the count without attempting to crawl over one of us. "If there was enough moonlight, they might have docked at Bugel, in Ighelun, and sent a message back over the border here to Welz, where there is a cavalry station. If they moved spritely. Or it could be the essential malice of my house staff—though I believe they would rather live, on the whole."

"They are cavalry," I called behind me, leaning out and squinting as best I could with eyes that used to be sharper. "Lighthorse, I believe, and regional, not crown. There's no gold on the harness. They are drawing toward us, but not at any great speed."

"How many?" asked Navvie.

I admitted I couldn't tell: somewhere between six and ten. The count tugged me back inside the coach. "Please spare the rude peasants the sight of a man hanging half out the window of a noble's vehicle. Whether they are six or ten will be of no matter."

"You have a great respect for our fighting abilities," said my daughter. "Or none at all," I added. Then it occurred to me he had not said he would support us or even be neutral in a confrontation between the soldiers of his government and us. He had never expressed any but a pragmatic unity with us, born of the moment's need. That need was now over.

"I would venture that this little troop is combing the roads for foreign spies," Dinaos said. "Spies that happened to survive being thrust ashore at twilight from a leaky, Harborman coastal tub."

"Why not?" asked my daughter. "They sent assassins into our house in Canton. When that didn't work, Lord Sibold himself came to the university."

The count sniffed and rubbed his shoulder. "So what is Sibold, that you should have been afraid of him? A simple baron, an inadequate swordsman, a brute without art . . ."

". . . the leader of a cadre of spies and cutthroats, whom we know to be after our lives," I concluded for him.

"Exactly. That's why you ought to have spoken with him. You might have learned something."

The sound of the hooves drowned out his words. Dust rose in and around the coach. "I think we're about to learn something now," I answered.

"Stop the carriage!" The voice had not the accent of Dinaos, but it spoke in Cantoner, not Zaquash. We had scarcely slowed when the count was past me with his face out the window. "Do so and I'll roll your head down the road," he shouted, either at his unfortunate driver or the lieutenant on the tall bay gelding. We joggled on.

The bay horse backed hurriedly across the roadway. There was a pause, and then the lieutenant said, "Forgive me, Count Dinaos. We had no idea you were within."

"Yet it is my coach, poor as it may be, with my coat of arms on the door, is it not?"

"Yes, but you . . . we didn't know you had returned to Eslad Province."

Count Dinaos was almost lying across my lap by now, and I

would find it very hard to draw. I glanced to the other side of the coach, where Navvie had drawn the tattered curtain over the window and was very still, pistol resting in one hand and dowhee in the other. I had not even heard her move.

"Well, why should you?" asked the count with a clearly false bonhomie. "Am I to tell you of my movements? Do you suspect *me* of being a spy?"

The lieutenant kept pace with our coach. I could catch glimpses of his leg and the horse's side. Then he leaned over the beast's neck and I saw his face. "No, my lord. Of course not. We're looking for a couple of Harbormen, a man and a woman, who may have been let off a boat recently."

Still, the count did not move. My legs were falling asleep. "Oh, lieutenant? How do you know this?"

"Sources," the man answered stiffly, and then he saw me. For a half-dozen paces of the horse, he said nothing, and neither did I. The count finally got off my lap. "Well, I have no Harbormen with me, so go about your business and stop raising the dust."

The lieutenant tried several times to speak before he could control his voice. "But my lord, who is that with you?"

The count's affability was now no thicker than a straw. "Ah yes! These two are none of your business. May I present to you Lord None of Your Business, and my Lady None of Your Business."

The lieutenant was a frightened hound, but he was a hound. "I must examine these people, Count Dinaos. I must command you to stop."

The affability disappeared. "Command all you wish, you stinking lackey! But what effect you think it will have upon me, I don't know. Your Regional Guard has no authority over me or mine: not my person, my house, my estate, my people, or my coach. If you dare to detain me you will not simply die, fellow. You will die in a manner of my invention, and I am known for being inventive."

Now the head and the horse disappeared from the window, and there was a confusion of horses and voices behind us. "They can simply shoot thought the wall and have done with it. If they have handguns," said Navvie, but her voice was calm.

The count sank against the squibs of the coach, groaning and favoring his shoulder, which he had somewhat mashed against my ribs. "They can if the lieutenant is willing to murder me. But if so, he must then kill his entire troop, elsewise at least one will eventually betray him and he will be pulled by horses, flayed, and sectioned." Stiffly he undid his belt and, holding his rapier by the scabbard, pounded the pommel into the roofboards. "Faster," he called to the coachman. "Make those sorry beasts remember when they were alive."

The jarring of our progress increased, and the count wedged himself between Navvie and me for support. Out of the window I saw the lieutenant draw up again, but he did not speak.

"They could simply kill your driver," whispered Navvie, who followed the cavalryman's progress with her pistol.

The count sighed. "The punishment would be no different. My body or my property."

I heard one of the horses coughing. It seemed terribly significant. I listened for unevenness in the hoofbeats in front, but four horses made too complex a rhythm to follow. The dust in the air worsened. The road seemed to grow worse.

Navvie had the hardest time remaining in her seat, for she had so little body weight. She clung to the frame of the window with one hand and the front seam of the seat with the other. This failing, she extended both legs and braced them against the opposite seat. I remember how her long skirt bounced, billowing through the interior. "You know, Count Dinaos," she said meditatively, "my departed mother would have forgiven you anything but your treatment of your horses."

He grunted and made use of both of us for his own stability. "Your mother was an unusual woman, Doctor." His eyes narrowed and he looked directly at my daughter. "What should I do, then— stop and wait for these yokels to lose interest in us? Would your mother sacrifice your own life to rest four scrawny nags?"

Navvie kept hold and answered between clenched teeth. "It is because they are scrawny she would not forgive you. You simply forgot they were here?"

"Not exactly," he answered, his voice broken with a gasp as we hit the largest obstacle yet. "It is merely that I have more than I . . ."

As we regained the road after our brief flight, there was the crack of something wooden breaking, followed by a grinding below, and then a terrible jarring as the horses slammed into their harness, the harness into the singletree, the singletree into the kingpin, the kingpin into the coach body, and the coach body into us.

"The off rear wheel bearing." I identified it.

There was an ill-bred cheering outside quickly squelched by a shout from the lieutenant.

"The axle is resting on the floorboards," said the count pensively.

There was a knocking on the near door. "My lord count, you must stop," called the lieutenant. "Your horses are dragging the coach by main force."

With a courtly bow of his head, Dinaos turned to Navvie. "Madam shall decide. Do we stop, as he suggests, or drag on?"

Navvie tried to smile. "Not even my mother would ask you stop, my lord. Drag on."

He pounded the roof with his pommel again. "Drive on, damn you," he shouted. "Drive on!"

"Master, I am afraid!" came the unsteady answer. I had never thought to hear a Zaquashman admit as much.

"All the more reason to drive on!"

There came a thump against the rear wall of the coach, barely audible over the grinding and the hoofbeats. It was repeated and followed by another, louder. The blows were heavy enough to jar us in our seats. The count cursed luridly. "Give me that," he said, grabbing for the dowhee I held in a loose grip. I did not see fit to argue with him. "Now, get over to the other side: both of you."

We did as he commanded and were rewarded by the sight of the Lowcantoner noble hacking viciously at the shaped panels of his own coach. First there was a glimpse of light, then a breath of hot dust, and then a ragged window looking out at the chests of horses.

The count bent to the hole even as two more blows rained around him. He put down the dowhee and pointed through the opening. "You. And you. And you. You are all dead men. Before the week is out your flayed bodies will be covered in flies in the tanner's market at Welz. And your lieutenant for allowing this to happen." His voice was just loud enough to carry, and it was very cold. The horses dropped back from our window, and there was no sound but the increasing grinding of the wheel and the worsening banging of the wheels on the road.

Suddenly there was a shrill cry from many throats, and I bent to see the entire troop coming forward at us, sabers raised.

"Now they have nothing to lose," I said. I picked up my dowhee and wondered what kind of fight we could make of it in this wooden box. Navvie was leaning out the window, her pistol in hand. She would certainly take out the lieutenant before they closed with us. Would they lose heart without their leader? Could she load again before we were reduced to close-fighting?

"I wouldn't worry about it," said Dinaos, or rather he began to say it. There were three hard, even bumps beneath us, and one of the floorboards sprang up like a whip, missing my nose by inches.

The pursuing horses were close now, but for some reason coming no closer. A few swords were thrown like knives, one of them sticking into the edge of the hole Dinaos had made, where it vibrated alarmingly. The cavalry faded behind, as did some of the dust. The coach shuddered to a stop. I heard a horse coughing.

"Well, that was the border," said Count Dinaos.

I dared put my head to the window, only to meet the eyes of a soldier in different uniform. "Please step out of the vehicle," he said in very poor Cantoner. I looked behind me, first.

There was a wind-scoured wooden barracks and a small building with a peaked roof. Except for the fulcrum-balanced gate across the road and an orphaned little stretch of fence running fifty feet to either side of it, there was nothing else of human provenance in sight. Unless, of course, I were to count the angry, milling cavalrymen very close to the other side of the gate. As I watched, the long chestnut tail of one of the horses whipped over the white wood and that part of the Lowcantoner cavalry, at least, was in Ighelun. Soldiers, dressed in the dry-grass color of the little country's army, pointed at this, and there were some high words exchanged, which the wind didn't bring to me. I got down and reached to help the count, whose face was sick and sweaty after his wood-chopping. He grinned like a shark.

"Count Dinaos!" The soldier backed away and his Cantoner became incoherent. He gave the universal signal of one index finger in the air and ran back toward the buildings.

Navvie came trotting around the front of the coach. "Be careful, my lord, Papa. They may have a gun or bow after all, and we are well within distance."

The count, looking fierce and martial in his victory, pointed to a knot of Ighelunish regulars hauling something into the road close to the gate. "Someone has a gun all right, my lady, but it isn't that turncoat cavalry of mine."

It was a small cannon, but it seemed modern and in good condition. As the cavalry troop noticed it they divided, hugging the edges of the road on dancing horses, and they waved their sabers tauntingly.

The artilleryman drew a couple of iron pins from the cannon's carriage, and the long brass barrel caught the sunlight as it swiveled toward the left, where the Lowcantoner lieutenant had gathered some of his men. They sprang to the right of the road and the cannon barrel followed. Spinning and cursing, the entire troop retreated along the highway, shaking their useless sabers.

"It was the miserable road that let me know how close we were to the border. Within a hundred yards or so, the people refuse to do repair work. It is as though they feel their duties are attenuated by the nearness of a foreign power. And the three bumps are directly under the gate, to prevent the border from being forced by speed at night."

"It was very close," I said, putting an arm around Navvie's shoulder.

"It was wonderful," Dinaos answered, sitting himself heavily on the coach's running board. In the weariness that follows crisis, we watched a man march smartly toward us, wearing a goodly amount of gold with his Ighelun tan uniform.

"It may not be over yet," murmured Navvie.

My knowledge of military uniforms was very out-of-date, but the wreath and two bars on the epaulet had once meant major. I said as much to Count Dinaos, but he returned, "It doesn't matter what he is, my friend. It is only important that he knows what *I* am."

And indeed, the fellow gave Dinaos a sharp glance, my daughter and me a duller one, and bowed smartly, clicking his heels. "Count Dinaos Proulin of Norll and Eslad?"

"Yours as always, Major," drawled the count, still seated.

"And these?"

"My party."

The major spared hardly a glance for us. "Count Dinaos, I must ask you what this has meant—those men chasing you."

Dinaos lifted his dark, heavy eyebrows. "Is there some question of my welcome in Ighelun, Major?"

The major blinked and then shook his head hurriedly. "You misunderstand me, my lord. But if there is some question of trouble with your own government, is it not better to let us know now?"

Dinaos got up. He made it take a long time. "Why, my lord, you're wounded," said the major.

"One of my first pleasures is dueling, Major. The occasional pinking is accessory to that. It keeps me sharp.

"But let me tell you that *you* misunderstand what you have seen. That rabble on horseback is not Lowcanton cavalry, but outlaws in fancy dress. At least four of them have been judged and condemned to be sectioned. When caught. They assaulted us on the highway where no man could see."

This, at least, was the truth. All of it was truth, if one considered that the count had the power to outlaw, and to condemn to torture and death at whim. The major was willing to be convinced. He nodded even more forcefully. "If you will be so kind as to sign a paper to that effect, Count Dinaos . . ."

The count bowed his head graciously. "I am going to my house in Bugel. You can bring it to me there." He climbed into the wrecked coach again and sighed gustily. "Get us a trap or wagon from my property on the south side," he called out. "I am going to take a nap."

Property? On the south side of what? Bugel? Where was Bugel from here? I ran to the horses, with the idea of pulling one out of harness and riding away in three directions at once, when Navvie pulled my sleeve. "He means the coachman, Papa."

I watched the Zaquash servant disappear into the dusty distance, bouncing as he rode the high-stepping trotter bareback. "What's to bring him back, my lord?" I asked. "Ighelun has no slavery."

Dinaos opened his eyes in irritation. "Ighelun has no slavery but neither has Lowcanton any wall around it. Any borderman with ambition ran long ago." He closed his eyes again.

Before the early winter twilight had fallen, we were aboard a light, open carriage of two seats and riding into the town of Bugel. The architecture was Rezhmian, though the people were generally taller and larger-boned than my mother's kind, and the language was nothing like. I had never studied it and rarely heard it spoken, for Ighelun is very small country.

The ground was still rocky, but here there were locust trees and a kind of squat oak that held its battered leaves through the winter. There was also a good attempt at agriculture. We passed a vineyard, where the vines were thick around as a man's thigh and trained on low fences to shade their own roots.

"This place doesn't make a lot of wine, but it's very good," said Dinaos, coming out of his slumber suddenly. "Some of it is fermented under pressure in the bottle, and some fortified."

I asked him how his shoulder was doing. "It hurts more, and I want something to drink," he said. With a wary glance at my daughter he added, "Something nonmedicinal. But no matter. We'll be at my house within a half-hour."

I didn't say anything, having had some little experience with Count Dinaos's houses, and I didn't say anything again when the pleasant, two-story housefront came in view, in neat red brick and white trim, with ranks of glossy windows and a carriage drive edged with evergreens. I said nothing but I almost wept in relief.

Here the servants greeted him at the door. Since they had warning of our arrival, there had been time to begin preparation of a lordly dinner. Before this, there were large tubs, and many hands to draw the water. While I soaked, these same hands washed my clothes: all of them.

Navvie and I were served our dinner alone, the count keeping to his bed, and afterward, we went out into the evening garden, where there was running water and fittings of alabaster that shone like white flowers in the last light. I left my daughter staring at the ornamental fish, with some questions in her mind as to whether they were asleep. I went into the rose garden, which was in this season a circle of black branches and large thorns. I felt rather like the roses, and I sat myself on the marble bench in the center. It was cold to sit on, even through my borrowed woolens.

Powl Inpress, earl of Daraln, was sitting next to me. I turned in surprise and the thought came to me that we were the same age, he and I. Perhaps his mind was working in that channel, for he said quietly, "Tell me which of two men is dead—the one who changed, or the one who stopped changing?"

I opened my mouth, not knowing what I would say, but he was quietly gone.

I was very tired. I sat as composedly as I knew how, because Navvie was approaching, and things were hard enough on her without letting her know her odd father was becoming still more odd. She sat behind me on the end of the bench and rested one hand on my shoulder. "I remember him as bigger than that. Of course, I was a child."

"What?"

"When Powl died. I was a child."

I turned on the cold marble. I noticed her breath made clouds in the air. We were not that far south, and it was winter. "You saw him?"

Navvie nodded. "Very clearly." She did not ask me whether he had spoken, or if so, what he said. I was tempted to ask if she ever heard the voice of her mother in conversation with me, but I feared to know the answer. We got up and went indoors.

No one in Bugel knew very much of what was happening in Velonya. Ighelun is a little country that suffers the influence of its large neighbors, Lowcanton and Rezhmia. It has no weapon except to encourage these two against each other, and the difficulties of the northwestern kingdom were important to them only inasmuch as they might be used for that purpose. I spent the next day and evening seeking information and another ship.

The best information I got came from my second search, for in Port Bugel I found out that the packet ship *Nananie* had docked the morning previous, with twenty-two passengers and five crew, and twenty-six stories of what had happened aboard it. The one man who had no story, the tongueless Sieben, had something better in the sealed authorization of Count Dinaos. The company had supplied a local captain and one extra sailor, and they had gone again, leaving the ex-pirate behind. No one knew where he went.

I also learned that the shipping line was cutting short its trips around the Morquen Sea and avoiding Velonya altogether. There had been violence in Morquenie and a threat of confiscation of foreign properties. There were smaller companies that still ran short-line service between Morquenie and Rezhmia the City, and I was told these were crowded now with civilians fleeing Morquenie.

A man behind a little pine desk in a square pine building on the wharf itself told me these things, and added the unsubstantiated rumors that the fighting was heaviest in the East and North-Central parts of the country, centered on the duchy of Norwess.

"Why do you say 'Norwess'?" I asked him, leaning on the desk so I would not fall.

He gave me a dubious look. "I say it because that's the name I was told. I think it's some kind of sectarian dispute. Why not Norwess?"

"Why not indeed?" I answered, and I thanked him for his time, and I went out onto the wharf again. I stood by the sparkling water in the strong northerly wind and considered Norwess and its sects, and that it might be better if I threw myself in. But I would probably have just swum to shore at the first shock of cold water. I am not suited for suicide.

I thought that on my way back to the count's holding I might do a small favor for Dinaos, who had done so much for us. I went from tavern to tavern (Bugel had two) looking for Sieben, but I didn't find the count's pirate.

■ ■ ■

This household, bought by the count's father only forty years previously, was so different from the ancient seat of honor he possessed in Eslad—and so much more comfortable—that I felt a burgher's satisfaction in the success of the commercial over the noble. My years in Canton Harbor had worked this change in my politics—or perhaps it was that most anti-aristocratic aristocrat, Powl. But what if we had come pelting in to discover that commercial reverses had caused the count to lose this pretty property, and we had sat in the road before the custom house with nowhere to go? Then we'd be beggars, no worse. Nothing new.

A beggar is no more like a burgher than he is like a noble. I resolved to keep this fact in mind.

That was a day of three good meals, and the count was rested enough to join us for supper. He seemed to feel no uneasiness over the absence of Sieben, and only the slightest irritation that he hadn't his painting to contemplate. Had he felt stronger, he said, he would have wanted to try me in other poses, other backgrounds.

I found the artistic personality interesting. I noted that he rearranged the ragout on his plate into a series of shapes, with the slivered meat in strips neatly across the bottom and the horsebeans scattered individually across the ceramic sky like fluffy clouds. I waited to see what he could accomplish with the salad.

"Nonetheless," he sighed, "I do not recommend that you stay for my recovery. If assassins found you in the Harbor, they will have no difficulty locating you here. And the border is open."

"It will have to be a new set of assassins," said Navvie demurely, but with a pigheaded set to her jaw.

"Yes, Doctor," said the count with exaggerated respect. I watched him eat the clouds off the sky, and then assault the earth.

"But I think you would run out of energy before my government—or perhaps your own—runs out of assassins."

"I think we ought to leave tomorrow, my lord," I said, and he raised his fork with a turnip promontory on it to stop me.

"Don't tell me where you're going, Aminsanaur. I am a loyal member of the Senate of Houses, and if someone were to ride up and tell me my guests were adjudged enemies of the crown, I might be put in a difficult position."

Navvie, like me, was watching the count's pictorial dining, and she raised her blue eyes only momentarily to ask, "Would that be different than the cavalry stopping your coach to arrest enemies of the crown?"

"Nobody stops my coach," he murmured, making emptiness out of the creation on his plate. "Nobody but the god of break-downs, to whom we are all subject."

The salad was of pickled long beans and beets, and more suitable, it seemed, to nonfigurative design. Or perhaps his con-struction was supposed to be a clock face. That would be suitable, under the circumstances.

"My lord Nazhuret," the count said after his plate was redrawn to his satisfaction, "I would be grateful if you would wait upon a sick man in his rooms tonight for a while."

I nodded, wondering what he didn't want Navvie to hear. Suddenly I was certain the man was going to ask for her hand in marriage, and I began to sweat.

"What's wrong, Papa?" she asked me, once we were alone again. I was picking through the house's library. Most of the books seemed to predate the old count's purchase, and were in Ighelunie, which language I scarcely could understand spoken, let alone in antique, smudgy black-letter print.

"A hundred things, of course." My hands found a volume in Allec, which seemed a medical treatise. Or a cookbook—I don't remember. I showed it to Navvie.

"Then let a hundred things go. You can't cure them by being nervous. Or so you tell me."

I sat down in a leather chair, which surprised me by being on hidden rockers. "The count. Do you trust him yet? Do you like him at all?"

Navvie found nothing interesting in the book I showed her. She snapped it shut impatiently. "I am inclined to like any man who saves our skin and then invites us to dinner. As a matter of fact, Papa, isn't it true that women in Canton do not usually eat at the same table as men?"

I put a foot down to stop the chair going back and forth. "The politeness of the courts is much the same from country to country, I've found. The Lowcanton noble who subjects women of good family of other countries to his local indignities would make more enemies than he can afford to keep."

"But how many foreign women of good family visit that fusty old country? And, if it comes to that, am I a woman of good family? I mean . . . we are eccentric, Papa."

I found myself rocking again. "I imagine the count is inclined to respect my family who saves his wet and wounded skin," I said.

I gave him an hour and then knocked on his bedroom door. He was abed with a sketchboard propped on his knees, chewing the blunt end of a charcoal pencil. He saw me and flung away the top sheet, and I saw a very careful drafting of one bedpost float across the room. "Sit in the high chair," he ordered, and for a long time he said nothing else.

It is easier to keep still when seated than at full attention with dowhee outstretched. It is easier to keep still after dinner.

After ten or fifteen minutes he asked lightly, "Is that the 'belly of the wolf'? Where you have been these last few minutes, I mean?"

I blinked. "I guess so. I don't use that phrase much anymore. Where did you learn it?"

Instead of answering he motioned me back into position, and there we were for another fifteen minutes. At last he put down his knees and commanded me to fetch the fixative and roller from the far table. "You'll get the stuff all over your sheets," I told him, but I did as he said.

"I have already got charcoal dust on them. Now it will not spread, is all." The sharp smell of lacquer filled the room.

"I got the phrase from your book," he said. He displayed the sketch. It gave me eyes of a depth and intensity that I do not possess, but I suppose that is art. I did not criticize, but I did tell him I had never written a book.

"Your series of letters, then, which was no doubt published without your permission, Unfortunate, but there it is. I read it. So did a number of other people."

Though he had put aside the sketchboard, he still chewed casually upon the charcoal pencil. Now not only were his fingers multicolored with stains of oil, but his mouth was surrounded by a gray smear. Despite this, the count looked in no way comical, but very intimidating. "You know, fellow, I don't know whether you would be in more or less trouble, had those letters to King Rudof not seen print."

"I am convinced that many people would be in less trouble but for Jeram's enthusiasm," I said spitefully, but he shook his head.

"The unknown can disappear so tidily, into a grave."

"I aspire, rather, to disappear tidily into the living world. And that my daughter, who has no connection at all with those letters, should be hounded by officials and assassins alike . . . It offends me."

"Is not at all fair," the count said. "What is?" He slapped the pencil down on the bedclothes. "But I don't want to talk about your daughter, my lord Duke of Norwess and Aminsanaur in Rezhmia."

I took one breath of relief. One.

"It is you who interest me, Nazhuret of Sordaling. Nay, you fascinate me, and have since I glimpsed you squatting like a heathen in the bow of that depressing little barge.

"You rouse my art and my instincts," he said, his dark eyes hot. "I want desperately to possess you."

Before I could reply to this surprising statement, if indeed I was going to reply—if I was ever going to find a word of my vocabulary again—he continued. "But here I am, punctured like a paper target and weak as paper also. So you can close your mouth and go your way and wonder how you have managed to misunderstand me so thoroughly these past days."

I mumbled, "Navvie told me I was misunderstanding you. . . ."

"For the last time, I don't want to talk about your daughter, but you. Remember I have read these scandalously intimate letters, and I know that you gained a poor respect for the sexuality of men and men by being made to suffer as a boy. That is your misfortune, and you will never understand yourself until you overcome that. And isn't that your great endeavor, my barbarian philosopher—self-understanding?

"So. When we meet again I may be in better shape to challenge you: in this manner, or in others. Things may not be better, Aminsanaur, but they will be different. Good night. Good-bye. Don't wake me when you leave in the morning."

We did not wake him.

■ ■ ■

It would have been so much easier if I had dared to take the coastal boat the rest of the way around the turn of Morquen Sea to Rezhmia. Six days and we might have been in the rose-colored old walled City, among friends I had known for over twenty years. It was too much of a gamble, however, and we could not depend upon being aided by a world-renowned swordsman twice in a row.

Instead we had horses from the count, which were waiting for us saddled and bridled when we left the next morning. The steward made us feel we would be subjecting him to his master's ire if we refused what Dinaos had ordered for us. I promised I would get the beasts back, but I didn't say when.

Had it not been for the state of my poor country, I might have been happy on the slow journey east and north, for the horses were good ones and the weather stayed dry. We had gold to buy food when hungry and fodder for the animals, and there was the occasional inn to break the monotony of sleeping on the ground.

Ighelun is pastoral, and all the sheep and cows have bells. I remember that plodding journey as having the sea on my left hand and a great tintinnabulation and baaing upon my right. There was also a lot of fog.

Eight days into our travel we came to the great river Aen, which descends from the Transmont Range and creates a belt of lush green in East Ighelun, dotted by towns and cities. At the brown delta of the river rose Plaerie, which in its gray stone walls and little round turrets looked remarkably like my home, Sordaling.

Here there was a school, which Arlin and I had visited once, riding south and east from Rezhmia. I could not remember the name of the dean nor yet that of the arms instructor my lady and I had met those many years ago, but we didn't need acquaintance to make acquaintance (as the saying goes), for the place was surrounded by taverns: student taverns, sailors' taverns, taverns frequented by people speaking Ighelunie, taverns where Rayzhia was the norm, and others so polyglot most conversation was done by hand signal.

After finding an inn that had livery service, I left Navvie and made a brief circuit of the various hospitalities, looking for one where Navvie could drink an ale without having to kill three men for the privilege. It was not a sailors' tavern, nor yet one of the students', but finally I discovered a place where the bartender was an ample, red-haired woman, and where citizens of both sexes gathered to talk.

I tried out its beer, standing at the bar.

"There's chairs," the bartender said Rayzhia, and I replied that I'd been sitting all day. She continued to stare.

"Are you gone gray, man? All gray already?"

I put my hand to my hair, wondering if it could be true, with all that's happened to me. "If so, Mother, no one has told me."

"Then you have very unusual coloring. The face of Rezhmia, but not the hair." She leaned forward. "And I suppose you can see all right, too. That's not cataracts?"

I almost spit my beer. "Mercy, woman! Surely you have seen a blue-eyed blond before in your life!"

"One or two, I'd guess. One or two. But they were towering, horse-faced people—not civilized."

"I am glad I am civilized," I answered her. "Old, perhaps, and with bad eyes, but civilized." If she understood my sarcasm, she didn't show it.

That evening, when Navvie accompanied me back to the

place, the talk in the barroom was not of war in Velonya, but of the drought. To travelers, it is fair weather; to country people, it is drought. This was supposed to be the rainy season in Ighelun, but most of the area's famous round limestone ponds were drying, and many stockkeepers had to haul barrels of water from the Aen daily for the cattle. Even the sheep could not keep going without supplement, for the grass was dry. The price of beef was down, as men culled their herds, and by that complex law which ties the fate of man to the fate of beasts, many people were out of work.

I tried to turn the conversation to politics, but the others at our long table were two drovers and a butcher. There was no hope for me.

"There's no sense calling this a misfortune," the butcher stated, punctuating his remark with the clang of a tankard on the battered wooden boards. "What is one man's difficulty is another man's fortune. Sometimes two men's. Now we have meat, plentiful and cheap. Even the poor can afford it. Had the rains come on schedule, what would they be eating this winter? Buns and onions, that's all."

"I like buns," I answered. I did not particularly like the butcher. "Especially with poppyseeds, hot and dipped in honey. I like onions, too, but buns are more satisfying."

He looked down his nose at me. "So you say, but if you had ever had to spend your winter with bread as your staple, whether with honey or without, you'd get tired enough of it."

There was no possibility of informing this comfortable Plaerieman, with his gabardines and his great silver buckle, just what varieties of hunger my daughter and I have endured, both the chronic and the acute. Nor would he have been interested, had I the words. Some imp of mischief, however, prompted me to say, "I never have had too much bread yet, nor honey, nor even onions. But during the long winters in the western forests, when most of what we ate was what we could kill, I grew heartily sick of red meat and crunching bones. *And* tired of the way it binds the guts together."

Whether it was my insult to his occupation, or my vulgarity at the table that did the trick, I had succeeded in offending our butcher. He rose in majesty, tankard sloshing, and retreated to the bar. The drovers, who seemed by their faces to be brothers and who had not opened their mouths yet, rolled brown eyes at me like cows themselves.

"I didn't mean to drive everyone away," I said to them. "I had just had enough about one man's misfortune and another man's fortune."

Still they said nothing.

"What my father means," said Navvie very gently, "is that we are people of Velonya and have been a long time away. We hear there is misfortune at home and hoped to get some news here, but all we hear about is the drought."

I was inclined to resent being so clearly interpreted, by Navvie or anyone else, and beetled my brows a bit. But the leftmost of the two drovers opened his mouth.

"Well, little miss, I can understand your feeling. We may worry about our livelihoods, here, but none of us is lying down dead yet."

"Is that what is happening in Velonya?"

"Humm. There's certainly refugees. I see'd um. Far east as the Old City in Rezhmia. And it usually takes killing before there's refugees, don' it?"

"What are they fighting about?" My twenty-seven-year-old daughter put her hands in her lap and widened her eyes until she looked about five. Both bovine brothers expanded under this treatment.

"It's politics," said the rightmost one. "It's always politics, when there's fighting."

"It's religion," said the leftmost one. "When it's religion, it comes to killin' easy."

"So. What exactly is the politics of the fight? The religion or the killing?" I asked, trying to remain calm and unthreatening so that we would not lose these two. "On one side we have the prince, now king, and the queen mother's party. On the other side . . . ?"

The drovers whispered and squinted and nudged each other.

Then the leftmost spoke for both. "The rebels have some dukes, I think, and some soldiers who won't follow the new lad. They're fighting under the banner of The Wolf."

"The Wolf?"

"Whoever that is," said the drover, and he shrugged.

It was a bad night, but my nightmares did not involve Velonya, or wolves, or even death itself. I dreamed of Count Dinaos, and the dreams were most confusing. I was glad to leave sleep behind.

"Where are we going exactly?" Navvie asked me at breakfast. "It can't remain your secret forever."

I apologized, and said I hadn't meant it for a secret. It had been only too uncertain to talk about. "To Rezhmia City, my dear. Where there seem to be refugees. I want to talk to them."

She cut her hotcakes with surgical skill, while saying, "But no matter what the refugees say, you will then have to cross the border, won't you? To Velonya."

"I don't know why you think that of me."

"I don't know, Papa. Inspiration, I guess." She dropped her knife and fork with a clatter, and I raised my eyes. Navvie is not a clattering sort of person. "You are going to try to leave me behind. It is not going to work."

"I don't even know that I'm going. What on earth good could I do?"

"You'll know at the time," she said, and she picked up her fork and her knife again.

■ ■ ■

I don't remember much about the horse I was riding, though I spent all day for at least three weeks on his back. There was a time when I would have remembered such a thing, and not only because Arlin would never have let me forget a horse. When I was young the world around me was a piercing thing, in good and bad senses. I was always either drunk on my own reality or bitterly stung by it. Each visitation, whether it was a visit to the school by a patron, a visit to the observatory by a renegade and thief, or a visit in dream of the parents I never knew or a royal visit in borrowed clothing, came inexplicable and unique. I reached many understandings this way, but I was almost always in trouble.

Now life tends to hit me like a dull drubbing on the back, and I have to work hard to keep my eyes open to the world. I hope I have succeeded to some extent. I stay out of trouble now for whole seasons at a stretch, but I have lost all memory of that good horse.

■ ■ ■

"What did he say to you?" asked Navvie. We were well into eastern Rezhmia by now, riding within sight of Morquen Sea under a gray, heavy sky and a slick wind.

I had not been paying proper attention, and when I realized what she had said I felt my face grow hot. I had been hoping she would never ask me about Count Dinaos. I was trying to think of a better answer than "I have no intention of telling you," when she added, "Powl. When he appeared in the garden, what is it he said to you?"

My mind changed gaits in midthought. "How did you know he said anything?"

She pressed her horse close to mine. Hers, I recall, was a bay. "Because he was Powl. Never the sort of person to make a trip just to show you his new waistcoat. Nor to give you a kiss for past's sake."

"No. He gave no kisses, for any sake," I answered, and the conversation seemed to be edging toward the difficult again. Dinaos must have read what I wrote about my complicated feelings for my teacher. I wrote too honestly, having no idea that anyone calling himself my friend would put my words into cold print.

"Powl said, 'Tell me, who is dead—the one who changed, or the one who stopped changing?' "

Navvie turned her face forward and rested both hands upon the pommel of her saddle. We rode on for a few minutes.

"That was certainly Powl," she said at last. "Do you have an idea about it?"

I had thought about my teacher's words, when not occupied

with assassination, war, and my own unpredictable nature. "I remember that when I returned to him after my first season alone—that was when your mother took me up on her mare and ran us back with the idea of saving him from the king's rage—he said that he probably already had changed his mind about half the things he taught me. He said it lightly but it hurt, because I had worked so hard to learn. This sounded a lot like the same thing."

My daughter shrugged. "Being dead seems to make for a lot of changes."

"Yes. And I haven't died for a very long time," I said. "And things do change more slowly as one gets older."

She yawned and shifted in the saddle. "I truly hope so. But remember, Papa, dying is not always an appropriate action. And change takes care of itself."

"I truly hope so," I told her, and the conversation was over.

■ ■ ■

We saw the city of Rezhmia two days before we reached it, sitting as simple and perfect as a child's dream on the mountainous horizon. The first time I entered that City, it fell down around me in a great convulsion of the earth, and though I have spent years of my life within its pink, rose-marbled walls, it is still to me a place of infinite, frightening possibility.

A few miles outside the gates we saw our first refugee camp, a place of forty people, many of them with dandelion hair like mine, and most of them much taller. This settlement was not only poor but slatternly, with a sewage pit right behind the mildewed canvas tents and dirty-bottomed children in the cold. I halted my horse and stared, for never in my years had I seen Velonyans living like this: the Zaquash camps outside Morquenie, yes, and those of the Sekretie people who have given up their icy homes to pick through the southerners' garbage, but never my stodgy western farmers. I was unaccountably embarrassed, and then grieved to think I might have had something to do with creating this.

We did not speak to the residents, and they had no way of knowing we were fellow countrymen. As we trotted down the road among the tents and shacks, one big blond stuck his head out of his tent flap, and he hefted a long billet of iron. I pushed the side of my horse close to him and put my hand to my dowhee, and he vanished under the canvas again, but as we rode on someone threw something, which landed between our horses on the road.

"Why should they resent the Rezhmians?" Navvie asked me. By her expression, she had not been so shocked by the sight of displaced Velonyans. "If they have been allowed to enter the country and pitch here in sight of the capital, they have been granted more than people can expect from a foreign nation."

"People aren't reasonable when their lives are in ruins," I answered her. "And anyway: perhaps they weren't mistaking us for locals. Perhaps they knew exactly who we were."

"Now you are getting conceited, Papa. They didn't know you."

There were crowds in the sprawling New City outside the gates, and many of these looked more Velonyan than Rezhmian, but there have always been many people of Velonyan ancestry (and language) residing here. I could not see any difference. I saw no more than the usual amount of poverty.

When we came to the east gate, however, I was surprised to see a guard station. The gates of the Old City had been open for the last twenty years and more, so that the distinction between the Fortress City and the commercial center had begun to blur.

Two women in good silks passed by the guards without receiving attention, but we were stopped smartly by crossed pikes, and our names and business demanded of us.

I was in a quandary. I had very strong connections to the Rayzhia court. In fact, if I wish to press the matter, I am a member of the royal family—which is an extremely extended family and without much family sentiment—but with the border flooded and relations with Velonya undoubtedly chill, the Rayzhia court could be wishing me to the devil. If I were to use my patrilineal name, I would be another bothersome Velonyan.

Though the truth may not be always the best policy, it is the easiest. I announced myself Nazhuret of Sordaling: Rayzhia name and Velonyan "title." I did not mention any business. The leftmost guard stared at my face intently for a few seconds and then pulled his pike. The other man dropped his more reluctantly. Navvie followed me through without challenge.

Within the walls the City appeared much the same as it had for the past twenty years. There were the carved stone lintels, the ornamental trees in tubs, and the pools of very large goldfish. The occasional broken tower or cracked pavement reminded the visitor there had once been a ruinous earthquake, but for the most part the Fortress City was busy and prosperous.

We walked our horses to the commercial stables, and were very glad to get off them; though I don't remember the appearance of the horse, I do remember the soreness of muscle it caused me.

Most of the inns of Rezhmia are in the outer city, but there are a few houses that have gone from grandeur to taking boarders. We went to one near the court complex which was familiar to me from previous years, but it was under different ownership now, and strangers took our money without a smile.

Soon we would be completely without cash. Perhaps it was time to buy blanks for eyeglasses, or for Navvie to paint the sign of mortar and pestle on our window glass and be discovered by the sick. But this was Rezhmia, and that meant guilds and licenses. Perhaps we would be reduced to begging again.

But Rezhmia also meant tea shops, *The Journal Page*, and much gossip. After baths and dinner, we set out to discover the state of affairs.

The Kenrek was where I had left it: that place which announces itself to be the "world home of argument." There was no salient dispute as we walked in, merely a rumble of conversation and a smell of melted sugar in the air. Navvie had tea, and I, who would rather drink warm pond water than stewed herbs, took two cinnamon buns. There were a number of *Journal* sheets on the floor, undamaged save for the occasional footprint.

Velonya was all the news, but it was not good news, nor easily understandable. "A visiting gentleman from Morquenie reports that at least a regiment of Royal Artillery were surrounding the port and the Provincial Statehouse as of last week." Did that mean they were expecting attack from the water, or that Morquenie itself had been in open rebellion? No clue.

"Ekesh tax fund unavailable for Crown, according to Prov. Counc." I wasn't sure this was even related to the disturbances, but Navvie thought it meant the lakelands were leaning toward rebellion.

"Velonyie loyalists stand secure in Norwess Province." This one confused me. "Didn't they say back in Bugel that Norwess was the center of the rebellion?" I asked, and I passed the sheet back to my daughter, who read it with knitted brow.

"You know, Papa, I don't think they mean . . ." She stopped and turned toward the door, and then my ears, too, heard the sound of men marching.

They wore the royal silks of Rezhmia, so much like the dress of the Naiish archers in cut and substance, but with so much more elegant an effect. There were six of them, and in front came an officer, a captain by his shoulders and his faded rose-colored tunic. He stepped to the head of his men, looked around the suddenly silent room, and came directly to our table.

We were on our feet before he had halved the distance. "Behind the counter is the kitchen and the door stands open," whispered Navvie. "One leap up and then down and out. You lead, Papa."

"No," I whispered back. "I think it's all right. He's bowing."

"So what? You are an important man. They bow to noble felons just before they disembowel them, don't they?"

By now the captain was beside us, and our attitude was making him nervous. He glanced at our sides, clearly expecting to find weapons there, and his face reflected the color of his clothing very nicely. "We didn't mean to alarm you, Aminsanaur Nazhuret."

"A troop of soldiers marching in order is meant to give alarm," I answered, feeling peevish. "Otherwise they would walk like normal folk."

He cleared his throat. "It is only a sign of honor, Exalted."

I stared at him and said nothing at all. It is a trick I learned in Rezhmia.

He cleared his throat again. "Aminsanaur, I am sent to you with a message."

"Give it, then."

He glanced left and right, and the full teahouse was busily not looking at us. "Here?"

I nodded. "Our quarters are inconveniently distant. Speak, please."

"Then I am to say that your aunt would like to see you." He spoke all in a rush and then breathed heavily.

"Tonight?"

"Yes, Aminsanaur. If it is convenient."

Navvie frowned, then giggled. "Is that the sort of message you thought needed privacy, Captain?"

He stared through her politely, and then saw what a pretty girl he was ignoring. The captain became human. "Well, I can't know, can I, Exalted? It's better to be conservative in such matters."

I folded *The Journal Page* neatly and put it in my shirt to finish later. I counted out a tip for the waiter and put on my jacket. I noticed that neither the captain nor his troop had moved. "Are you determined to accompany us all the way to the Towers, Captain?"

"It is my honor," he said firmly.

"Are you equally determined to march? If you do, you will convince my daughter, the neighborhood, and possibly myself that we are going to our execution."

"We certainly don't have to march," he said.

My aunt was the royal mother and regent of the sanaur of Rezhmia, who was then about seven years old. She was not really my aunt, any more than the sanaur of my youth had been my grandfather. The family was so extended that relationship became unwieldy. I had met her three times before in my life, once since her son had been acclaimed the new sanaur. I remembered her as a woman of great common sense.

We walked through the dark streets, and despite their best intentions, the soldiers had a strong tendency to march. Navvie had an equally strong tendency to disrupt their marching—by hurrying forward and then stopping to retie her shoelace, by dropping her coin purse on the cobbles and having to quarter the street until it was found, by stopping at shop windows, and once, to my secret satisfaction, by skipping. She talked to them, too: the captain and the men, asking the simplest questions like a tourist, and by the time we reached the sanaur's household gates, she had converted one troop into seven individual men.

The sanaur's quarters were a concentration of all that is pleasant and civilized in Rezhmia. The walls were thick but dry and frequently wore egg-tempera paintings of domestic subjects, goldfish and cats being popular themes. I lived among these paintings for years and never wondered about their quality, but now for a moment I felt I was seeing them through new eyes. Count Dinaos's eyes, to be exact. I wondered if he would find these pretty murals beneath contempt.

Next to smokeless oil lamps, men and women sat reading. In Velonya the women would more likely have been doing embroidery or plain sewing, and the men . . . well, drinking beer, I guess, and not in a cozy parlor.

I saw no one I remembered, and the household very politely did not stare as we passed. Perhaps they were simply not interested.

We found my royal "aunt" in a chamber by herself, and she was doing embroidery. She paused her needle as we entered the room, and rubbed the heels of her hands over her eyes.

"There is not really enough light for this," she said. "But I promise it would be ready for Alie's birthday."

I bowed and Navvie curtseyed. "Sanaur'l Maigeret," we said together. The captain departed without a word.

The sanaur'l was, like most of my family, rather short. She stood, taking the lamp in her hand and held it first to my face, then to Navvie's. "You are worn," she stated, and she told us to sit down.

"I am sorry about your friend, nephew."

It took me a moment. "You mean Rudof, king of Velonya?"

"Yes. I am very sorry." Her mouth tightened in a rueful smile. "More sorry than you can imagine. It may lose me my regency. It may even lose Nadell his crown."

Not so many years ago, it was very common for a young san-aur of Rezhmia to lose his crown, by the simple expedient of be-ing killed. The latest attempt upon a sanaur, however, was at least twenty-five years previous to this time. I had played a stupid part in this attempt, and a slightly more clever role in preventing the assassination. I hoped that Maigeret was not talking about murder.

"Because relations with Velonya are becoming strained?"

She sighed and crossed her neat ankles. My "aunt" is consid-erably younger than I, and did she not have to project the role of sanaur-mother to all the world, she might have passed for a young-ster herself. But she is not young-hearted.

"Because, Nazhuret, we will be at war with Velonya before the new year is out."

Out of the corner of my eye I saw Navvie reel in her chair. Had she not considered this possibility? It had been in my mind since I heard of the death of Rudof.

"You see, the new regime is weak and unsupported as of yet, and it is most definitely not our friend. Why would we wait until it has eliminated all dissension at home and is ready to strike at us with a combat-trained soldiery?"

"Are you sure they will strike, Sanaur'l Maigeret?" asked Nav-vie, though by protocol she should have kept her mouth shut in the presence of Maigeret.

The lady did not seem to care about protocol. "I suspect it. Others here are certain. Think, child: war is a financial gamble, but civil war is without possibility of gain. Before Rudof's death, the Velonyan army was moderate and professional. Now it has to be swollen by press and conscription, all of which will have to be supported somehow. An army assembled and in debt must attack until it is paid or destroyed.

"Besides—knowing that it is in the interest of Rezhmia to attack, the Vestings will feel forced to anticipate us."

It was in my mind to ask Maigeret who among the court was more certain than she of Velonya's aggressive intent, but my daugh-ter cut me off.

"What if the rebellion succeeds, Sanaur'l Maigeret? What if a new government reflects the policies of King Rudof?"

Maigeret looked blandly at Navvie. The sanaur'l was only a few inches taller than my daughter, and only five years older, but they seemed nothing alike at this moment. "Are you planning to revenge your godfather, Nahvah Howdlidn? Or possibly to set your father up in his place?"

Navvie wore a gambler's face that would have done credit to Arlin, but I could see she was startled, first to be accused of such temerity and second to find that the regent of Rezhmia remembered her mother's family name. "It would be late for that, Sanaur'l. After all the years he has refused Rudof's offer to restore Norwess, who would back him now in a claim for the whole nation?"

Maigeret nodded, as though Navvie had said something completely different. "The crown of Rezhmia would, granddaughter. About that all factions here agree." She turned back to me.

"With arms light and arms heavy and with our full standing infantry we will enforce and recognize your claim.

"There is the only success possible to your rebellion, granddaughter," she said to Navvie, and "There is the only hope for your father's nation," to me.

I was intensely angry all of a sudden, and did not know at whom. "It is not 'my father's nation' but my own nation, Sanaur'l, and I am not a Rezhmian tool."

"No. As it happens, Rezhmia is your tool at the moment, and not by our own choice."

I blinked, as though she had waved a fist in my face. "You think I am part of this rebellion, Maigeret? I had nothing to do with it. I have not been in Velonya for over two years."

"Yet it formed around you like ice around a rock in the stream. You are the philosopher, the iconoclast, a foreigner in your own land. Twenty years ago the blockheads in Vestinglon were calling you 'Rudof's sorcerer.' I remember that."

"I must contradict the sanaur'l. That was what they called Powl Inpress, earl of Daraln."

She shook her stubborn head. "No, that was thirty years ago.

I have paid some attention to western politics, against the chance this day would come. Listen to me carefully, nephew, and don't answer out of hand.

"These people have built their rebellion upon what you stand for and, in fact, around your name. Whether you like it or not—can you let them fail?"

"My dear aunt, such a plea unworthy of you! You don't care a turd for 'all I stand for,' whether science, philosophy, Velonyan justice, or Velonyan survival."

"Not a turd," she agreed, with a thin smile. "Yet I'm telling the perfect truth."

"I've never found a perfect truth in my life," I told her. "Or at least nothing I could tell to someone else." I stood up. "Am I under arrest, Sanaur'l Maigeret?"

"No," she said. Not "No, of course not," but merely. "No." Navvie rose with me, but turned again to the sanaur'l, frowning intently as though she would say something. I was afraid she might, and I dragged her along by one hand.

This time no soldiers accompanied us through the pleasant chambers of the Towers. Well-dressed people were still reading beside lamps that did not smoke. I envied them.

"Do you remember, Navvie, how the king's great-great grand-father—I mean Rudof's great-great grandfather—accepted the help of Sekret tribesmen to discourage the Felonk and Peleolonk raiders who had wasted the Sea Islands north of Vestinglon?"

"I know all that, Papa. Once you invite in the stranger you cannot invite him out again. But we still own the Sea Islands, don't we?"

"What 'we' is this? The language there is not Velonyie. The faces are not Velonyan."

She laughed and pulled against my arm, to slow my rapid stalk through the palace. "Look who is talking about a Velonyan face!"

The outer door was opened by a footman, who seemed to fear I would smash through it headfirst. Perhaps I would have. The cold air was a relief. There were stars in the sky, and (if I recall cor-rectly) a moon rising gibbous, its outline wavering from the heat of a thousand hearth fires. "So you think that at this late date we should throw aside all of Powl's teaching and embrace the affairs of nations? He said, 'Stay out of the reach of officialdom. It will be deadly to you.' He also said about me, 'He would not be a good king. Not in any world like this one.' "

"And he said, 'Who is dead—the one who changed, or the one who stopped changing?' "

Suddenly the cold was no relief; it froze me to the bone. "I have spent all my life, Navvie . . ."

"But don't listen to Powl, or whatever looked like Powl and sounded like him. Erase all of Powl for once, Papa: all the rules, the observations, the opinions. We are in the middle of something, and our inaction will cause as many things to happen as our actions." Her breath was making little silver clouds, and her face was white against the darkness. "Any movement of my hand, tonight, will ripple out in all directions. I feel it, Papa. I don't know what leads to what, but I know we're at the center of it all."

It was very quiet when she finished speaking, and I thought I could hear water freezing, crackling on the stone walls. "Everyone's always at the center of it all, Nahvah. Only sometimes do some of us feel it.

"I'm tired to death," I said, and we went to the inn without another word.

That night I had a dream in which I was back at Sordaling Military School, changing the beds. I did not know any of the people I saw, neither masters nor pupils, but I overheard a master in the hall outside the dormitory saying, "He's an old boy. A very, very old boy." I glanced down at my hands and they were white and corrugated. I left the beds and walked to the shaving mirror on one wall, in great trepidation as to what I might find, but in the rectangle of pocked and smeary glass I saw only the blue sky. When it occurred to me that I was indoors, and in a long dark chamber, I was so startled I woke up.

I didn't get back to sleep again that night, but waited through the darkness for there to be light enough to move about. I heard nothing from the hall except the bootboy returning people's shoes about an hour before dawn. That is how I know that Navvie must have left the inn fairly early in the night.

She left me a note. I don't have it word by word in memory, though I read it over so many times I should. It was to the effect that she had things to do, and they might not now be the same things I had to do, and so farewell for the present. There was something in the phrasing, or in the general audacity of it, that reminded me of her mother. She also asked me, very politely, not to follow her.

I was at the Towers shortly after sunup, asking to see my aunt the sanaur'l again. The first person I spoke to said it was not possible, the second said I had picked a very bad day for it, and the third who saw me was Maigeret.

"No, nephew. I would not make arrangements with your Nahvah behind your back. Such tactics would not work in the long run. Where do you think she has gone?"

Neat hands put a large breakfast in front of us. It seemed as alien to me as the runes of East Sekret. "To Norwess. That I know. To see Jeram, who started this whole thing."

"The young priest of the rebellion? Has she then a tenderness for him?"

My laugher was rude. "Tenderness? Good God, no. Or I hope not. No—he's just the center of this storm, and if anything is to be done about it, it is to be done at Norwess. She knows that much."

Maigeret glanced narrowly at me. "And so do you, apparently."

I was playing with a slice of melon as I talked. It was greenish-white like the crescent moon in fog. I wondered where the hothouses were that could provide such fruit in midwinter. "I may have less hope something *can* be done."

She nodded, feeling cynicism call to cynicism, or perhaps merely age to age. "But now you will have to go to Norwess anyway, to bring back your daughter."

I tried eating the melon. It tasted like midwinter. "No, Sanaur'l. She is almost thirty years old. And trained from childhood to be unobtrusive when she can and to protect herself when concealment is impossible. No woman in the North is better prepared for travel than Navvie, and few men. She should have left me long ago; I only regret the circumstances. I regret all these circumstances."

"So what will you do?" she asked me, as one might ask what a person will do now that the red boots he was going to wear are found to have a hole in them. She ate two hothouse grapes and didn't look up for my answer.

"I'll go to Norwess," I said, and then Maigeret did look up.

"I'll go to Norwess, but not to haul back my erring daughter. I'll go for the same reason she went—to see how things are."

I pulled back my chair and stood over Maigeret. That was not courtly behavior, but I was pressed for time. "May I have a good horse?"

The sanaur'l nodded. "You can have more than that."

"And if—when I return, say in ten days, if I decide I want the support of Rezhmia?

Maigeret also rose. "I can give no promises. Ten days may change a lot."

I said I didn't expect promises, and I bowed out.

Though I don't remember the horse on which I rode into the City, I do remember the horse on which I rode out the next day. More surprisingly, I remember clearly one upon which I refused to ride: the one presented to me by the proud court livery as a mark of favor.

He was a beautiful stallion, almost black in color, and despite the season, his own heat had kept his coat short, marbled by veins and tendons. He was awe-inspiring. "I killed one just like this," I told the stable manager, "on a run of about three days once, from here to Warvala. I have to go about half again that far, and I don't think he'll make it."

Horsemen all seem to take pride in never being surprised, but my words surprised this one. "Aminsanaur, he is the best we have."

I asked if I might look around and took his silence for assent. The stables were large, clean, and filled with elegant horses. Some of the stalls bore the insignia of private owners, and these I skipped by, but most of the animals were crown property and all were jewels. All bore lovely, firm, well-tended flesh and beautiful crests on their necks. I was very frustrated.

In the back two rows of stalls, where there were fewer windows and the boxes were smaller, I found animals of less evident breeding. And feeding. There was a half-clipped dun I considered, despite his white eye and bared teeth, and there were a few dusty bays with some of the blood of the Naiish in them. Almost at the end of the stable I saw a white glimmer in the shadows, and at my request out stepped a slender gray mare with a long neck, slightly lady-waisted and high on her legs. I stared at her and said, "Three faces of God!"

The stable manager was at my side. "That's just one of the messenger horses, Aminsanaur. They are nothing much. Their pedigrees are lost, or embarrassing. A mare without an honorable pedigree is of no account."

I asked him very politely to show her. He did so, dismissing her utility all the while. "You don't want a mare for a solitary, forced journey, Exalted. She may come in season and become unusable to you."

"In midwinter? That would be some mare indeed. Besides—I have ridden mares in season, and stallions in rut. Let's see this girl go." I took the rope lead and tied its end to the knot of the halter, then threw the loop over her head. She was not terribly tall, so I boosted up bareback. She did not have a back that invited such a style of riding. With the stable manager trying to clutch me back, I pressed the girl forward along the stall line. Her easy, springing movement was more of a shock than her appearance. I leaned close to her ear and whispered, "How many years is it that you've been dead? Twenty-five? Twenty-seven?" The mare turned back her head on a flexible neck and looked at me with both eyes. She made a sound that seemed to say she hadn't been counting.

"What have you been calling her?" I shouted to the stable manager. He answered, "I don't know that she has a name. She's only one mount in forty, in the courier service."

The mare was dancing in place in the dark aisle. Her tail made white ghosts in the air. "She's one in a million," I said. "Her name is Sabia."

It is quite possible that Navvie's departure had left me too alone, and since I had not been alone for some years, I retreated into the past at first opportunity. Or it could be (as the stable manager surely thought) that the old beggar-noble, always eccentric, had gone beyond the line at last. I traded Count Dinaos's respectable gelding for this wild gray shadow and rode through the pink city at a plunging prance, which relaxed to a canter as I let her go.

Sabia had been Arlin's youth: a slightly outlaw horse for a thorough outlaw. In my time I had been very jealous of Sabia. In her time the gray mare had shown her temper to me, too. She had been only fourteen when she was cut down by assassins; I had seen the whole thing.

Of course, this Rezhmian courier horse was not Sabia. I must say that now, or I myself will begin to think I am insane. But now that I have said it, I can forget it and relate how I said in her ear, "Sabia?" and she nickered in response, and how her back half seemed to float and flap like a kite tail in the wind while her front legs followed the bit. This behavior is not laudable, but it was Sabia's behavior, and neither training, discipline, nor heavy burdens ever made her change. I am not a fancier of horses, though I have had to ride hundreds, but with this creature I felt such a presence of my dead Arlin that I was half in love.

"Sabia," I whispered. "Let's go fast."

We were in the wine country by midmorning, riding through the gnarled, leafless vines and past hundreds of refugees in their hopelessness. Two men threw things after me—stones and curses—but they hadn't a chance of hitting at the speed we were moving.

All those years ago, a few months after the death of the first Sabia, we had done this same route—Arlin, myself, and the sanaur's own prophet. He had found us a shortcut right through a vineyard that cut away from the sea and straight toward Warvala. There was no possibility I could find that trail, if it still existed.

It did exist, and the mare found it. She leaned right, clamping firmly on the snaffle, which is the only bit the horsemen of Rezhmia recognize, and charged between two rows of vines no different from any other I had seen. I was forced to duck my head and close my eyes to save them from whiplike branches, and I hoped only she wouldn't run us into the winery wall, or off a cliff.

When it seemed we were clear of the foliage, I looked up to find we were climbing a stony hill and had left more than one field behind us. "Is this how the sanaur's couriers ride?" I asked her humbly, but she was too busy to respond.

That day passed swiftly, in more ways than one. It was not travel in the same sense as Navvie and I had traveled up the coast. If the mare's progress was breathtaking, so was my solitude. By midday, her gait had slowed—if indeed it was any slower—to a long trot, which did not seem to tire her any more than standing in her stall. As I seemed to have no say in where I was going, or at what rate, I was free to look about me, and to think.

Now that I had lost Navvie, I had lost everyone who was anyone to me in my whole life. I was remarkably cut off, remarkably singular, on the back of that rushing horse. I did not even belong to the ground. Most odd about it was that I was happy.

There is no wilderness within a day's ride of Rezhmia City, however fast the horse. Through the whole day we had been within sight of human beings or human works. It surprised me, therefore, that the sun sank upon us in a highland area devoid of shelter and without even a clear road.

Had the mare taken me all the way to the Bologhini Peaks? That was an impossibility. Nor had she taken me so far north that I was out of my reckoning, because the sun would have informed me by its angle. I did not know where we were, why there was no worked field or habitation thereabouts. I had a small stock of grain for the mare, but to use it up in one night left us vulnerable for the future. Yet this Sabia was not a spirit, to live entirely on memories, nor could she run on her own body fat. I gave her what I had, in small handfuls to prevent colic, and allowed her nose to find her a small runnel of water.

I did not trust the looks of the stream, but the stewardry of the Towers had packed me leather bottles of the Rezhmian new wine.

This specialty of the country can be stored only through the winter, being scarcely fermented at all. It would never be popular in Velonya, where people like their wine to hit them like a hammer, but to be just to my people we have beer and ale for travel.

I also found—as I recall—a waxed round of cheese and an assortment of breads, both hard and soft. I do remember dried olives, for I spat the pits into the darkness and the mare startled broadly each time. She never got tired of the game.

It was a cold camp, since not knowing where I was, I did not try a fire. We were under way with the light, the mare having shared whatever bread and cheese I had left. I still let her pick the way, for I was utterly lost.

The sun rose behind us and picked out the jagged teeth of the mountains ahead. We were not at Bologhini, but we were near it. I must have covered seventy miles that first day.

We would not go so far today because the going was a jagged trap, with stones lying scattered across the few flat stretches. I wondered how many of those stones had been left by the chain of great earthquakes of a generation before. I had been in these very mountains to witness the first few shocks, and in the City for the big one. How many passages had been closed by the upheaval, and how many opened?

As the heat of the day came up, and the hills increased their angle, I got down off the mare and tried to lead her. This was a miserable practice, for she was a ruthless bully on the path, and wanted to go faster than I. After losing a bit of skin and a bit of temper, I decided to grab onto her tail and let the idiot pull me. She was going where she liked, anyway. In this manner I sprang over the ground with considerable ease, though I had to trust she wouldn't kick me.

We had just scrambled down a broken hill face, where her speed had almost pulled me off my feet, when I looked at the pattern of rocks against the sky and I knew where we were. I lifted my eyes to the left and saw the squat domes of Bologhini a half-mile away. The mare broke into a trot and I almost lost her.

Bologhini is not easily accessible from the south road, and so has never had a strong Velonyan influence. Most of its people make their living somehow off the plains to the west—which is to say, they are Naiish by blood, though not always as bloody as the Naiish. I was disturbed to see the same squatters' camps spread on the high outskirts of Bologhini that I had seen around Rezhmia: the sad, inefficient attempt at nomadism by people with no talent for it. And I heard my native tongue spoken, shouted, shrilled, and wept- in, before my nervous mare even entered the town.

Here my face was to my advantage, but my hair was against me. I had donned the Rezhmian men's kerchief before entering Rezhmia, and now I stuck all my dusty locks into its dusty linen. My eyebrows were by now as much gray as blond, and there was nothing I could do about them, anyway.

Besides a horse, some wine and cheese, the stewardry of the Towers had given me money. I don't think I had ever had as much money in my pocket before, unless I was carrying it for someone else. I rode past the bubble-shaped houses and those strung up like tents, through a public garden all of water and colored rocks, and into an innyard that I recalled to have a good livery.

The groom looked distrustfully at the dirty man on a dirty horse. My accent, however, was of the best (Powl had made certain of that long years before) and as the man approached, he said, "I know that mare!"

"So do I," I replied, far too weary to explain. "She's come from the capital in a day and a half. She has farther to go. Please do as much for her as you can."

I took a room, but spent only a few hours in it, lying motionless on a bed, between sleep and wakefulness. I took a bath, ate, ordered a meal to be packed, and returned to the stable by late afternoon.

Sabia was resting her head on the stall door. Her eyes watched me. I filled her pack with oats again.

She had been washed down and brushed, and even her flying tail detangled. "You seem to like her," I said, tipping the groom.

He laughed like a Zaquashman. "The couriers call her 'Hazardous Duty.' But I don't have to ride her. I know she is as fast as a sinful thought. Where are you taking her?"

I was stopped for a moment. I almost didn't answer the man or gave him a lie, because what I was doing was so much like spying. But lies are inauspicious, as is offending a groom, so I told him "Norwess."

His sly face went sober. "For the crown?"

"Not officially."

He walked over to me and spread his hand horizontally below my eyes, to make a map of it. "Say this is the mountains," he began.

"You don't want to go down here," and he ran his left finger above the root of his right thumb, ". . . because the riders are gathered in the plains. They're upset, like everyone else about this thing with the snowmen. Also, they're robbing the refugees. They won't see you as any different. So run her up the crescent here until you reach the place the mountains dip down, beyond Cieon." The left finger moved along the crevice between his right index and second fingers, to the smallest joint, and then slid over and off. "Then you'll be far enough north that there's some trees, and if you don't mind the uphill grade, you've a straight west shot toward Norwess."

I thanked him and tried to tip him again, but he refused. "Not if it's for the crown," he said. I left without knowing myself if I had cheated the man or not.

I left Bologhini, and my horse seemed fresher than she had been in the Towers stable, and on the river-bottom road that ran north of Bologhini we made excellent time. About an hour after that we were ambushed.

It happened where the road was pitched by outcrops, during a time Sabia felt like galloping. I saw the string glinting across from rock to rock, but she did not let me pull her in or turn her. The impact took her just below the knee, and I did not try to stay with her, but rolled to be clear of her body. When I stood up again, I saw two young men running at the floundering horse, knives in their hands, and for a moment I thought I would see the death of Arlin's mare repeated across time. But this creature had her legs in the air, and they were pumping like those of a startled spider. The men had not succeeded in getting near her before I was at them, and with my own version of the Naiish battle cry I swung my dowhee within an inch of their faces. One ran and the other slipped and fell.

"What the hell did you want to kill me for?" I shouted in Velonyan, for this one by his long face and fair hair was obviously a countryman of mine.

"Not you, your horse," he answered me, in the broad accents of Norwess—my father's accent, I suppose. It is not mine.

For a moment I thought I was looking at a disgruntled crown courier, for whom Hazardous Duty had been too much. But no, there were no Velonyan couriers in the sanaur's service. "Why?"

"To eat it, of course," he said, and there was more resentment than fear in his voice. "We have had no meat to eat for over a week. Nothing but barley."

I stared. "You're not even thin! My horse should die so you don't have to eat barley? The people of Bologhini live on the stuff."

He stood up as though all danger was past. "The little peasants can do so. We can't. Our bones are bigger, and our . . ."

I touched the dowhee to his neck. "You don't seem to understand. I am angry at you. I don't like your excuse. I would like very much to kill you. I think you should run away."

This took time to sink in, and when it did his retreat was as slow and sullen as his speech. I led the mare a while, until I was sure her gaits were even, and then got up on her. Immediately she broke into a canter.

I'm sure there were refugees from Velonya who really were starving, but as it happens I didn't see them, and my feelings toward my native country were rancorous for the rest of that day. At evening we reached the little sheep town called Cieon, where the mare and I found accommodation.

When I left town the next morning, it was with a new set of shoes on the mare. Her feed bag was filled with Naiish-style fodder: dried fruit, lamb fat, and gristle. I find it unsettling to feed such stuff to a grass-eating animal like a horse, but there was no way we could carry enough grain to see her through, and she seemed to be used to such stinking fare.

By now it was cold: true Velonyan cold, and I feared that the gray skies might release their rain and do us damage. All day we descended the north cut in the mountain range, and by evening we were on the flat again. I had never come through this way, though once I had made the journey from Rezhmia to Velonya as far north as the Sekret steppes. Here there were scattered copses of pine and wind-twisted oak, and the winter-killed grass did not appear to have been grazed heavily. I hoped we would not meet herders.

I saw no people, though the trails were clear. I kept the setting sun in front of my left shoulder and trusted I would find Norwess eventually. I made a camp without fire, ate food not much different than the horse's, and wrapped myself in my blanket, wishing for stars. It was so cold within a few hours that I rose again, hauled myself onto the mare, and lay full length on her back, my face warmed by her mane. I stretched the blanket over both of us. I am not sure either of us slept in this position, but we were warmer.

Toward morning she decided to lie down, and I got off to let her do it. Once she was settled, I wrapped myself again and put my back against hers, and we both had at least an hour's good sleep.

I woke with a familiar smell around me, and found snow on the blanket and on my kerchief. The earth was dusty with the stuff and the sky was lead. The mare and I relieved ourselves, ate rank mutton and wrinkled apples, and got under way.

It snowed steadily, and still she went at her springing trot, her head between her knees to judge the ground. Perhaps her fall the day before had made her overcautious, but I let her go her inelegant way. Had she stumbled I certainly could not have pulled her up; my hands were under my shirt, in the waistband of my trousers.

Soon the snow was not a dusting, but a thick blanket. I don't know what trail we were following, if any. I could only guess the position of the sun.

I had been woolgathering for some minutes when I noticed that Sabia had found a track to follow. It was the trampling of an animal not too large—neither man nor horse—for in some places the wind had blown it into drifts where the mark of the beast's barrel was evident. As I wondered about it, I noticed large dog prints coming from the left to join it. I thought the dog left the trail again, but I stopped the mare and looked carefully. This was another dog, coming and not going. I thought about this. After a few minutes I opened my frozen lips to talk to the mare.

"Do you know you are following a wolf pack, my lady? Is this something the sanaur's couriers regularly do?"

She didn't respond. Since her nose was down there by the path, I assumed she could smell the beasts that had made it. I hoped she knew what she was doing.

The sun came out so brightly my eyes began to water. It was directly before me, so we had slipped our direction a bit. I tried to rein the mare right and out of the beaten trail, but she began to flounder and skid and pulled her head back to the opening the wolves had made. At this rate we would touch on Ekesh before Norwess and waste time going north, but the alternative seemed to be to wait for a thaw.

At noon, with the white caps on the pines sparkling and the snow crunching around us, we heard the first yip. The mare froze in place, her body as tight as a drum. She blew a cloud that crackled in the sunny air.

Another yip answered, ahead of us, and I saw a pale shape bounding through the snow, a hundred yards in front of us. The horse wheeled and almost fell.

I took her spin and made her continue it, until we were aimed back the way we had started. I knew the position of two animals already: one to our right and one ahead, and their intent was clearly to drive us. I had only seen three sets of tracks, but three were enough to drive the mare until she fell, and I with her. I would not be driven.

I have never kicked a horse as hard as I did the gray mare. I think the energy of my heels drove her up and forward without any involvement from her brain. As she leaped, I was drawing my dowhee, which I almost dropped from my clumsy, cold hand.

I was cavalry trained from the age of five. This style of war has been made obsolete in our lifetime by the perfection of powder weapons, but I did not think the wolves had powder weapons.

Had the mare been battle trained? I didn't even think about it. I threw her at the gray shape in the path before us, and I bellowed like a savage, brandishing my sword.

I don't think the wolf had prepared for this. Perhaps the human smell had not even reached it when it decided to attack the big prey. It pivoted and ran up the path again, while behind I could hear the other two doing what they did best: chasing something that ran from them.

I had to reach the first before the others reached me. A horse, like a wolf, wants to chase anything that runs from it, and wants to run from anything that chases it. Consequently, the mare was of my opinion in this matter, and she was a very fast horse.

We were only a few yards behind the gray wolf when he bounded off the trail and started breasting his way through the snow sideways to us. Without my urging, the mare leaped after.

The wolf hit a pocket and disappeared down to his neck and ears, and as he floundered, I leaned over the mare's neck and sliced his throat open. He screamed once, and between that sound and the spray of blood, the mare reared and spun. Had I not had my left hand wrapped in her mane I would have been spilled.

Her front legs came down in the wolf trail, and I used her fear to propel her back toward the other wolves. There were two, as I had counted. One was as gray as the first, and one was dirty white.

They, too, had heard the death scream of their pack mate, and neither hunger nor the thrill of the chase could overcome the fear of the monster they saw before them. They turned tail.

I might have let them go, but something in this experience had made me as savage as they were. The mare was not so happy about chasing this time, but she, too, was afraid of me by now, and she ran at my command.

The wolves did not try to separate; perhaps the sight of what happened to their fellow in the deep snow made an impression on them. Wolves can run, but no wolf could have outrun that mare in a sprint. We caught up with the gray first, and I gave Sabia my heel to swerve her left so that I could take the creature as I had the first wolf, but she did not respond. Instead she did what a horse hates to do—she ran the animal down and trampled over it. I heard the crack of bone and felt the unevenness of her footing, and then it was behind us, and there was only the white wolf, running with a very red tongue dangling.

It made its move to the left, away from my dowhee hand, and when I had controlled the plunging mare and sent her into the snow after it, I found the creature on its back, wagging its tail feebly. It was a male, like the first one, but pissing itself and grinning at me.

I was acquainted with a wolf once, or a dog that was much like a wolf. Or perhaps it was a particularly vile kind of ghost that I knew. I have never known.

The mare was blowing under me. Her heart was a drum and her hide black with sweat. I led her fifty feet away and wrapped the reins once around the branch of an oak. When I returned to the white wolf, it had righted itself and wiggled its way toward me like a puppy, its ruff giving it a very puppy face as well. With a single stroke I cut its throat, and then in a fury I do not understand I hacked the body until there was no way to tell what color the beast had been. I had never done such a thing before to any creature, animal or human.

I dried the mare as best I could with my woolen blanket, and laid it over her to retard the cooling. Both she and I were rose-stained from wolves' blood. I walked through the snow and led her, a long gray furnace, wrinkling the air with her heat and sweat. By the time I got on her again, we had both calmed down.

Sometime in the middle of the afternoon we found a road, unmistakable even under the coating of snow. The good thing about it was that it led the sinking sun back over my left shoulder. The bad thing was that it was not an engineered Rezhmian road, nor even one of our handcrafted Velonyan thoroughfares. It was packed earth that twisted around trees, with only the most wheel-breaking stones removed. It was a happenstance sort of herders' road, and I was doubtful concerning the herders that might have made it. Yet it would be worse to find no people at all in this northern wilderness, for the wind blew from the north, out of Sekret, and it had all the way from the eternal ice to build its malice.

When cowpats were seen dotting the snow and human and horse tracks multiplied, I thought it better to pull Sabia wide, hoping to scout the settlement or camp before they had a look at me. The mare disliked this; having found the road, she was satisfied with it. We were plunging in place when a boy trotted our way on a pony as thick and furry as the dust under a bed. He had a broad face, like the children of the Naiish, or for that matter like most children in the world. He watched the battle for some moments as the mare swung her head and neck with such force she threatened to break her skull against a tree, or against my skull. Then his pony trotted its tiny steps toward us, the boy flicked out a rope, caught Sabia over the nose with it, and dallied her to the horn of his pony's saddle. She reared once and the wide pony lightened on all four of its feet, but if there was any response in its face, the hair hid it.

"She is too green for you to be out here alone," he said to me chidingly, in Sekret. I barely understood him. Then he added, "She has hurt herself. And you, too."

I looked at the rawhide rope over her nose and found no damage, and then I realized what we looked like, the mare and I. I pulled together what Sekret I remembered and answered, "No. Three wolves we killed. Not we hurt."

He gave a bass grunt he must have learned from an older relative, pivoted his pony, and began to lead us along the road. Since this was the way Sabia had insisted upon going, she made no demur. My reins were locked against her head by the noose around her nose, so I went along like a sack in a pack train.

I smelled smoke. It made my stomach growl. I was reasonably glad the boy wasn't Naiish, though I have more experience with the Naiish culture than the Sekret. Experience does not always build fondness, yet I reminded myself I might be as easily killed by strangers as by old enemies. Still, my stomach growled.

I tried the language again. "She is not green," I said, or hope I said. "Nor is she fresh. We have ridden from Ceion this morning."

The boy turned his face to me and succeeded in hiding his expression as well as the pony had done. Still, he stared at the gray mare for a count of five before starting off again. "I have not yet been to Ceion," he called over his shoulder. "Is it as great as they say?"

"I liked it," I answered with perfect honesty. "I was warm there."

We turned past a stand of coated pines and the smell of cows hit me—of cows and latrines. The camp had probably begun the day under the same white pall as all the countryside, but the activities of a few dozen humans and at least a hundred cattle had turned the earth to cold muck.

Still, it was interesting. Despite my weariness, my frozen state, and the dried blood that stuck to me everywhere, I gawked and stared. In a way it was like Bologhini, the domed city, though here the domes were built of blocks of snow. In another way it might have been one of the winter camps of the Naiish, with its cattle palisade of sticks and dry briar. The stone fire-wells were like the camps of my own people, and in this land of trees they were blazing even in daylight.

The cattle, though, were like nothing else. They were scarcely larger than goats, and wide as the boy's pony, and furrier. Their horns rose up and then forward in a businesslike manner, though many of them had the ends sawed, and some were blunted by balls of painted wood. All of the beasts were fox-red.

We came to the middle of the camp, and people began to gather around us. Leaning forward, I slipped the noose off Sabia's nose. She snorted, and immediately started to shiver. I got off.

The blanket I had covered her with was now frozen stiff. I could not even unfold it. I looked around me at the curious, sunburned faces of the herders, and because I could not remember the Sekret word for blanket, I shouted "Shirt! Shirt for the horse!"

They had anticipated my mare's need, and two women were already scurrying through the foul snow with wool rugs padded with horsehair. I tried to strip off the saddle, but found my fingers had lost all feeling, and so even that was done for me. Sabia was covered from poll to tail and led broadside to one of the fire-wells. She took it all as her due.

I, too, was blanketed, and in friendly fashion was prodded into one of the snow houses. Inside, the light was blue.

There was a fire going within. It was a very small fire, but still I wondered. "Why doesn't the house melt?" I asked the woman who knelt beside it, but she giggled and scooted out the leather door flap.

"It will melt in the spring," said my boy guardian gravely, and he took my hands in his and regarded them. There were two grown men in the hut with us. He spoke to one of them so quickly I could not understand, and the man followed the woman out.

"How many wolves did you say you killed?"

I repeated for him that I had killed three, by driving them into deep snow.

"And that horse let you do that?"

I felt a need to defend my mount. "She is not usually as you see—as you saw her. I was trying to avoid your village and she wanted to stay on the road."

"She has good sense," he pronounced.

The people were as kind as any I have met. They fed me and the mare. They gave us a little snow house of our own, with a leather roof. The mare, with her fine, short coat, needed it as much as I. They asked no more questions, not even where I was going. Perhaps my inadequacy with their language made them think the effort hopeless.

I was more curious, or perhaps just less polite. I asked questions of everyone I met: the woman who brought me water to wash, the girl who brought me dinner, and above all the pony boy who had adopted me and—at least as he thought—saved me from a wild horse.

I found out they were northerners, whose practice it was to come this far south when the freeze made the ground impassable to the wagons of the Naiish, their enemies. The scrubby cattle could get sustenance from lichen on rocks. The people's boast was the cattle made some use of the rocks themselves, and as I myself noticed stones and gravel in the ever-present cowpats, they may have been right. The main home range of the people was hundreds of miles north of here, but in the winter even Sekreters could not make a go of it. Hence these tropical latitudes.

I asked the girl what her people called themselves, and she told me her name was Etha. I asked the older woman the same question, and she pointed to herself and said, "Two sons, one daughter." The boy merely shook his head and made a dismissive gesture. Perhaps the herders did not have a name for themselves. Perhaps the name was secret. Perhaps I had asked an entirely different question by error.

In the middle of the night I was wakened by a man clapping to announce himself outside my hut. I pulled the flap and he came in, accompanied by viciously cold air. "I am Horlo, and I have been seeking strays. I came from the morning side. I found your three wolves. One was no good from hoof damage, but here are the others."

He handed me two pelts, stiff as boards from the cold. "Horlo, I thank you, but I abandoned these. What is abandoned belongs to him who finds it."

He shrugged, but what a shrug means to these people was not entirely what it means to a Velonyan. "You had no choice but to leave them. Your horse was wet. I heard the story." He forced them into my hands almost belligerently. I thought fast.

"Still, I cannot take them, my friend. I travel fast tomorrow, and the smell will frighten my difficult horse. You would do me a favor by making use of them."

This gave him pause. "I will give you something for them, then," he said and went through the leather flap before I could object.

My friend the boy returned, blinking sleepily. "So you told the truth," he said. "You killed three wolves from a horse, in deep snow."

I felt overly praised. "It was the deep snow that made it work."

He nodded. "Yet it is an uncommon thing. Your horse is uncommon too. I shall have to apologize to her for my rope."

He stood in dignified manner until I realized I was supposed to leave him alone with the mare. I went through the flap myself and frozen air assaulted my nose. The sky was clear and the stars crackling. After a minute, he came out again, and I felt the urge to confide. "I am from a northern place, too," I said.

He gave me that precocious stare. "Anything you say, I will now believe," he said, and he walked away through the snapping snow.

The next morning I was fed again, and so was the mare. The people looked at the coins I offered them as though they were so many buttons, but that may have been pride as much as ignorance. Horlo had found his payment for the hides: a rough woolen jacket padded in the chest and back with channels of cow hair. It turned out to be the warmest garment I have ever owned.

When I was on the mare again, he stood in my path and said, "You should know that one wolf still follows you."

I stared down at him. "Why? How do you know?"

"I know because I tracked you. Why? I don't know the mind of a wolf. They have good hides, but their souls are a defilement."

I thanked him for his information, and I left the camp not knowing its name.

The mare was not so sprightly today. Perhaps the Sekret fodder disagreed with her, or perhaps even she had her limits. We trotted on at a good rate, but on this leg of the journey we would break no records. The sky remained clear but the air was no warmer, and the light had my eyes weeping by midday.

My Sekret jacket had mittens attached, as we at home will provide for small children who lose their gloves. These mittens had no thumbs, but a slot in the palm for the reins to enter. I wrapped my blanket around my legs and the mare's barrel, keeping us both a little warmer. She pulled no nonsense on me today.

By afternoon the horizon had changed shape. There was a bulge ahead and over my right shoulder. It did not look like mountains, but rather as though the earth itself had a swollen bruise far away. I recognized it as the beginnings of the highlands of Norwess. From now until our journey's end, we would be climbing.

I failed to find a road that would lead us by a more direct route, though there may have been one under the snow. Sabia seemed inured to the work and I myself was numb, body and mind. We passed another herder's camp, but this one was deserted: a congeries of humps in the snow. Before sunset we came to the border.

First there were hoofprints marring the white surface perpendicular to our path. There were a number of them, going in both directions, but there was nothing else to be seen. Next came a road marker, cut in granite like a gravestone. I almost didn't get off to wipe it clean of snow, because I wasn't sure I would be able to climb back on, but I had to know where I was.

The side I cleaned was unmarked, and I stared at it dumbly for some moments before it occurred to me the writing might be on another face. I cleaned the whole block, to find that on the south side of the thing was written EKESH TERRITORY and on the opposite side NORWESS PROVINCE. As I squatted there, a man on a laboring horse trotted up and used his animal's legs to press me against the stone.

"Where are you going and where did you steal that horse, peasant?" said the soldier in uncultured Rezhmian. I reached fingers through the slot in my mitten and pinched the heavy bay's foreleg skin, causing him to dance back. I stood slowly.

"Though you did not ask me my name, fellow, I will give it to you. I am the Aminsanaur Nazhuret, grandson of the Sanaur Mynauzet, and nephew of the present Sanaur'l Maigeret. The mare was the gift of Maigeret and my business is my own."

I have so much the look of the reigning family of Rezhmia, along with its lack of size, that this has been an inconvenience to me at times. This man, however, was not the sort who looked at faces, but at clothes. "You're going to die for that impudence, pig!" he shouted.

He drew his saber as he pressed his horse sideways to me. I darted under the animal's neck, drawing my dowhee as best I could in the mitten. The horse danced back from me again, and I sliced upward between its front legs and severed the girth.

The soldier, who had been leaning heavily in an effort to reach me under the horse's neck, suddenly heaved with the saddle and hit the ground shoulder first. The saddle hung sideways between breast-plate and crupper, and the beast, with its nasty cut between the legs, bucked screaming away.

Before the man could rise, I jumped with both legs on his chest and put the edge of the dowhee to his throat. "Now do you believe me, you son of a slave? Could a peasant have done this to you?"

He was not thinking, not even of his own survival. He pulled a good-sized poignard from his belt and stabbed twice at my ankle, causing me to dance on his chest. I kicked him in the chin, but I was so clumsy from the cold I could not knock him out. I took my dowhee from his throat and sliced his hand off. Red blood pumped into the snow and my mare, tied to a pine, looked at it with only remote, weary interest.

"Now let me tie that up quickly or you'll die," I said as the fellow sprang to his feet, screaming much shriller than was his horse. He did not even staunch the wound with his left hand, but held the horrible thing out before him and ran into the fields of snow.

I followed as best I could, but my legs were frozen and over-used. By the time I caught up with his bright trail, he was face downward in the snow and there was no more blood pumping.

I floundered back to my mare and got on her. I had to check that my feet were in the stirrups, for I could not feel them at all. I took the road that ran between Ekesh and Norwess as fast as I could make her go, before other border guards came. They would be no more willing to listen to explanations than this one had been.

Now, after fifty-five years, I had finally announced myself to be royalty, and had immediately to kill a man to enforce my claim. As Powl said it would be. What would Powl think of me?

At least he could not say I had ceased to change.

■ ■ ■

Fir branches brushed my head and made me aware of my ker-chief. Having just created of myself a Rezhmian aminsanaur, I decided to put him away again. The cold bit at my ears, but bare-headed I was no longer so recognizable as a foreigner. Of course, being a foreigner in a country at civil war might be an asset. I folded the kerchief and put it carefully away.

In my life I have been in nine countries, not counting the various principalities in the Felonk Islands, but I have never seen a place more beautiful than Ekesh Territory. The hills are gentle, the farms rich, and the waters many and clean. Now these waters were thoroughly frozen, but I did not want to test any ice with the weight of a laden horse, so I kept to the road and let the inviting white countryside be.

We began to pass these rich farms, and with the snow cover so even, I could not tell whether strife had hurt them or not. I looked for marks of passage, and first I saw the occasional hoofprint, traveling with the road or perpendicular to it, and then I saw the boot prints of people, and then I began to see people themselves. So gently did I enter my own country and culture I marveled at the number of years I had been away from it; nor did my first sight of it convince me that there was trouble here.

At a crossroads I saw a row of shops, and behind one frost-dotted window was a saddle. The price was not exorbitant. In the doorway a man was standing, looking out the glass top of the door. I suppose he was desperate for entertainment, for he stepped out and called, "You oughta feed that horse!" Then he laughed, in a manner to cut the offense of the remark. I did not reply.

None of the buildings were inns or liveries, so I couldn't take the man up on his suggestion, and it was too early to be giving up the day's travel. But I took the right-hand turn of the cross-roads and within a few miles had begun to notice the climb. I was in Norwess.

Five miles later we passed a burned building, too badly ruined for me to tell what its function had been. Sabia gathered enough energy to shy at the smell. I didn't know what to make of the damage. Had there been aggression, either of troops or rebels? Had people been burned to death in this black shell? Enough houses went up in smoke in a peaceful winter because of fireplace sparks; I didn't need to invoke the god of war here.

The ruins were capped in snow, and the surrounding snow was

bumpy with half-obscured footprints. No great evidence of horse. I rode on.

I came to Longfield just as the mare and I were used up. I would have preferred to stay the night in a smaller town, but at least here there was choice of accommodation, and warm stabling. I gave my name as Timet Glass.

Another guest had reserved the bath when I arrived, but the manageress said if I wasn't too proud to use soapy water I could warm up in the tub for free. I accepted her offer, and treated the hot water with great respect. I had been a stranger to both cleanliness and heat for too long. My cracked hands seemed to be locked onto invisible reins; I swished them through the water until they relaxed. My hair I scrubbed under the pump. My one change of clothing was Rezhmian silks, so I manufactured a history for Timet Glass while I soaked.

There were only five of us in the public room that evening, but there was talk enough for a multitude. I needed to give only three pieces of information about Master Glass: that he sold optical supplies in both Velonya and Rezhmia, that he was born in the west of the country, and that he had been away from home for a long time this trip.

It became the duty of the other men and the barmaid also to bring an old exile up-to-date. The difficulty was that no two of the guests had the same idea as to what had been happening this winter in Velonya.

One man—a poulterer, I think he was—told me that the old king had been killed by mushrooms, which will happen eventually to anyone fool enough to mess with them, that malcontents with foreign influences had chosen the event to try to undermine the succession.

I saw the barmaid lift her head at this, but she said nothing. She really had no opportunity to speak, for another fellow, whose name and occupation I do not remember, said, "Mushrooms? Mushrooms? I never heard her called that before, but I guess the name fits: pale and deadly as she is."

The poulterer slammed his tankard on the table and sloshed

good ale over us all. "You'd better tell me who it is you're talking about, you braying ass, and it had better not be who I think it is!"

The third man, who was slight and dark and had expressed an interest in playing cards, caught my eye and said, "Well the truth is, Master Glass, we've been having a dusty winter in Norwess, and no doubt. There's not much you can say that won't start a fight these days."

"My fault entirely," I said, and with one foot behind his knee, I sat the poulterer down in his chair again. "I ask awkward questions and of course I get awkward answers. Just tell me what roads a peaceful man should avoid to keep out of trouble."

"Avoid them all," grumbled the poulterer. "The Wolf is all over the heights. They'll strip you naked and leave you in the snow."

The slight man spoke up. "The king's infantry held most of the lowlands until the last freeze. They did a bit of burning as they retreated. Probably they'll try again as the weather improves."

"It's not going to improve," I said with some certainty, though I don't know where my information came from. Perhaps it was the instinct honed in a man who has spent too many winters without fixed abode. The poulterer drank that part of his ale he had not splashed out, rose heavily, and left us in anger.

We played does-o for hours. The slight, dark man was a cheater, not a very good one. I had been trained by the best, but I let him win a little Rezhmian gold from me, in payment for his information.

That night I heard howling, but when I sat up in my bed to listen, I had the peculiar sensation that what I had heard was part of a dream just broken, so I listened again, heard nothing, and fell back asleep.

Though I was not raised in Norwess, I have spent enough time there to know the roads, and most especially, the slow, bad roads. I picked the slowest, worst, and most meandering and used it to head north, in heavy-falling snow.

In this portion of my journey, a horse of less speed and more knee action would have served me better, for Sabia was continually misestimating how high she had to raise her hoof on the long climb, and we stumbled. But to do her justice, she hadn't stumbled on the passage of the Crescent Peaks, so perhaps her clumsiness meant that this intense work had finally gotten to her. It had certainly tempered her energy, though she was still more horse than I was used to riding.

I passed through that zone of maples only ten miles or so from the former oratory where I had lived for almost ten years with Arlin and then with our daughter as well. It is a pretty place and dear to me, but I did not go out of my way to visit. The maple zone is rich-soiled, and the farms are clean and compact, but the first couple of buildings I rode past had been burned. There were frozen bodies scattered under the snow: not human, but of Sabia's kind, and also a few goats. The mare snorted and groaned as she recognized the horses. I was a little less nervous.

Norwessen farmers seemed too rich to be revolutionary, and too hidebound. I found it difficult to believe in a rebel horde that could attract them, so I was forced to believe in a rebel horde that burned them. The prints, though, declared that troops had been by here. Too late, perhaps?

We were passing the second ruin when I heard howling again. I do not say wolf-howling. The man who claims to distinguish the howling of a wolf from that of a domestic dog is a rare woodsman or a liar. It made my poor mare trot faster, whichever it was, and it chilled me so that I drew up the hood of my jacket.

The first howl was answered from my right-hand side, and I lifted my arm behind to check that the dowhee would slip easily from its pack. Sabia seemed to understand this gesture, for she gave her biggest groan yet.

I looked around us and saw nothing but shining white earth and dull gray sky, with silver trunks of trees stitched between. My eyes dazzled from the brilliance as I tried to focus; I wished I had equipped myself with smoked glasses. The mare did not appreciate being stopped. She swiveled back again and trotted on with all the speed the ground would allow.

It seemed I had chosen wrongly in taking the unobtrusive

road, for we were heading nowhere but into darker woods, as pine began to replace the maple. I wondered if the mare's huge heart and lungs were feeling the altitude yet.

The howling repeated itself, ringing in the emptiness, and after a half-hour or so was replaced by the yips of a hunting pack. Sabia gave a stiff little buck and I myself cursed. "You have food in plenty, you stinking butchers," I addressed the beasts. "Whole frozen horses. Cows, probably. Are you so spoiled you can't waste your effort on frozen meat?"

I did not hear the right-hand voice again, but our behind-follower was faithful. We did not stop for luncheon, nor to drink, but were driven up into the evergreens, where I know Sabia was feeling the thin air. The sun came out. Shadows of trees confused the path. There was a farm off the road, and it was intact by the look of it, but no tracks went in or out, not through the three layers of snow. I kept to the road.

Now the rocky bones poked out of the earth, and the going was even worse. I could not see ahead or behind. The mare dropped her head to gulp snow, but she needed more water than that. I gave up hope we would reach a town and resolved to meet the pursuers on the best terrain I could find.

A place where the road cut through a cliff provided cover from the back and one side. I pulled in the horse but might as well have been pulling in an equestrian statue. "Here, Sabia. It's the best we'll get!" I said, but she had other ideas. She broke into a gallop.

I looked behind and something was running, pale, down the road. It shone in the sun.

The cut through the rock was behind us now, and in front was a slight decline to a valley filled with men. Some of these had horses, most had not. They had come down from the North, turning snow to mush, and rooted up the frozen dirt for a rod's width. I saw signs of organization among them. All were armed. They were very, very many.

All this I saw in a moment, and then I grabbed the right rein in both hands and put all my strength into hauling the mare around.

The dry leather snapped, and Sabia bolted forward like a racer when the rope drops. We were among the men, and I remember the sweat smell of them after the cleanliness of wind and snow. They probably noticed my sweating horse and me as well.

Since I couldn't stop the mare, I decided to drive her forward and through the crowd of them. I booted her and she leaped, slipped, skidded, and came to a stop on one haunch, with me still on her back. She clambered up again and shook her skin, rattling me and all my belongings.

Many men were staring at us. Having nothing better to do, I stared back. One fellow, with a head of yellow hair and a harquebus as old as I am, pointed to me and behind me. "The wolf," he said. "Look! It is the pale wolf."

I was still trying to understand this when I felt something touch my hand where it lay on my mare's withers. A cold, wet nose had been thrust into the reins-slot of my mitten, and leaning up against the mare, frightening her not at all, was a long, lean body of silver-white. I felt its affectionate tongue slide across my palm. Its ruff was wide, and its eyes triangular and smiling. On its face, throat, and belly were stains of pink.

I met its strange eyes and recognized them. "The last time we met, you never let me touch you," I said to it. It got down on all fours, danced about, and leaped up again. ". . . Or was that the time before last?"

As I muttered to the animal, I waited for the assemblage to become weary of talking about me and talk to me instead. No one did address me, though I lost interest in the wolf and my mare lost interest in standing still in the snow.

I looked around and I saw pieces of Norwess—the populace of Norwess, that is—imperfectly mixed. The ring of men closest to me seemed pulled together from some small town shop-row, while only five yards distant stood a recognizable mass of Provincial Militia, still in their uniforms and with sergeants attending. Behind them were the countrymen who had fled from Sabia's wild hooves as we charged into their camp, not mixing with the shopkeepers or the militia, and even the few women I perceived among the crowd were huddled together, shawl to shawl, as separate from the mass as so many nuns.

The resemblance of these to religious women stirred a thought in me. Since no one addressed me, I spoke to them. I caught the eye of one of the whisperers and said to him, "I'm looking for a man named Jeram. Jeram Pagg, of Worrbltown. That's Worrbltown by the Soun Falls at Ekesh line, south of here."

The fellow, who may have been a tailor or a draper or any one of a number of trades, squinted and stared and was incapable of any answer. Behind him another said, "Seek the banner, Your Grace. If Jeram has joined us, he will be with the silver banner."

There were a number of standards in this crowd, all of them furled. As I allowed the mare to wander, I counted heads as well as flags. Four flags and easily eight thousand followers. There was what must have been the red leaf of Norwess, borne by the militia; the swan of Velonya, borne by men in royal blue and white but with the badges of rank removed from their uniforms; a red-backed standard that I guessed to be the marten skin of Mackim, duke of Forney, who was now Norwess as well, and the fourth one, which I found amid an assemblage in undyed homespun, all with their heads bowed and all identically dour. This banner was very tightly furled, but unarguably silver.

"Excuse me this liberty," I said to the young man holding the standard. He glanced up at me somberly and then he stared. Forcing myself to smile, I took the staff from his hand and unlaced the binding.

Silk and silver rustled out into the dry wind. This banner was simple and painted by hand in black ink. There was the outline of a wolf, running, and in the middle of it, an irregular splash of ink, which drew the eye. The wind blew, the silver wolf ran. I felt the ludicrous impulse to run with it. For no better reason than this I thought of Dinaos.

"An artist did this," I said to the lad, but I could not hear his answer. With effort I took my gaze from the banner.

"Forgive my snatching this. I had to know. I come looking for Jeram Pagg; can you help me find him?"

"He is probably already back at Norwess Palace," the young man said. Carefully he rolled and cased the banner once again.

I sighed because that was still a long way away. I wondered what to do now, and it came to me I could get off the horse. It seemed humorous that idea hadn't occurred to me before. I slipped down from the saddle and slipped much farther than I had intended. Only the bracing arm of the young man held me from the trampled snow.

"I haven't used those legs lately," I told him. I stamped as feeling came back into them. The mare stamped, too.

The fellow was mumbling something. I asked him to repeat it. "I drew the flags," he said. "I mean . . . you seemed to want to know. Sir. Your Grace."

This was the second person here to call me by that title. It was very peculiar. "What? Am I a bishop, to be called Your Grace?"

"You are Nazhuret of Sordaling, if I am not mistaken. Sir."

He was a tall blond boy, square-boned after the fashion of Norwess. His face was more pink than white. "You say you drew the banner, lad? I like it. Not the banner itself, but the art of it. Art and insight, perhaps."

His face went more red than pink. "I am third level, Your . . . sir. On the path of the void."

"I have no idea what you are talking about," I told him, and I led the mare through the ranks of identical ragged beggars and went looking for anyone whose face I knew.

I found no one, but Duke Mackim, whose honors included most of Norwess, found me. When last I saw him, Mackim had been a lad of twenty years, quite bright and likeable. He had been interested in the dowhee, which was unusual for a Sordaling-trained man, and I had sparred with him cordially. That had been almost eight years before.

Now he was more than cordial. He pressed my hand warmly, and the look in his brown eyes would have done credit to a spaniel. "I have expected you these four weeks," he said, and he called for food and fodder to be brought out of his personal packs.

I took my hand back. "You expected me? How, when until this last week I had no idea to make the trip?"

"I knew you would come to the banner," he said with perfect certitude.

I almost told the man what I wanted him to do with that particular banner and all it stood for, but my attention was caught by the sword he wore in his embossed and silvered belt. "Are you making your living with a hedger now, milord?"

He faded back a pace. "I don't pretend to be your equal, Nazhuret . . ."

"It would be a peculiar standard of mankind in which you were not, Mackim. The dowhee's strength was not in dueling, anyway, but in breaking blades off to eliminate the duel. And it was useful because it was unknown and therefore hard to counter. But no more. The saber or the hedger—both relics of the past. Now we just shoot each other."

"There is more to the life of a warrior than that!" He rested his hand on the plain hilt in its fancy sheath, as though he would soothe a dog.

"Oh? I don't know what that would be," I said with borderline politeness. I did not look at him. The duke fed me, anyway.

■ ■ ■

This little force of humanity, which seemed scarcely able to move itself along the road, had already had two full encounters with Velonyan cavalry and had given far more losses than it had received. Velonyan cavalry could afford far more losses, but still the record was impressive. According to Mackim, they succeeded because they fought with reason and instinct, against the rote and drill Forwall, the Commander of Cavalry, had learned in school. I suspected they won partially because the rebels could live off the land and dissolve into the towns and villages when pursued.

Considering the weather, their camp was meager. There were not tents enough for all, and though they built fires, their wood was limited to what they could find, take by force, or pry from demolished buildings. The men who traveled under the banner of The

Wolf built no fires at all, but were warmed and fed at the fires of others.

"I wouldn't give them a thing," I said to Mackim. "Able-bodied fellows like that, can't they work for their bread? And for their fire, too?"

The young duke sat in the warmth of his own campfire and looked sideways at me. "They have chosen the path of perfection. Is it so different from . . ."

"Perfectly useless is what they are," I was being cranky, and I knew it, but it was complain or cry for me.

"They are the backbone of our fighting force, and deserve our care for no better reason than that. They ask no great thing of me—of us—no lands, no office or honors. Just food and a fire. Besides, Nazhuret of Sordaling: are you not the first beggar-warrior, and father to all of these?"

"That damned manuscript. I wrote it years ago. I lived it so long ago I don't remember the people involved. Damned Jeram has a lot to answer for."

Mackim smiled. "Then I wish he were here to answer you, instead of me. Discourse is not my specialty, though I admit to reading the *LENS*. Without it, none of us would be here, I think."

I looked into the darkness past the fire, where so many men slept, or did not sleep and wished there had been more to eat, or nursed wounds of war or wounds of the frost. I wondered where the dead were, whom these had left behind: stacked no doubt like cordwood, waiting for the cemeteries to thaw in spring. "God in three faces help me! When I wrote that I was honest, in my own way. How could I have been so misunderstood? Where did I validate war between nations, let alone against the legitimate crown?"

". . . Not legitimate anymore," Mackim interjected. "Not after parricide . . ."

". . . Do you really think Benar had any part in killing his father? What evidence?"

The duke's eyes glistened in the firelight. He looked at me with calm certainty. "The prince was too prepared, Nazhuret. Within two days of his father's death, he was oversetting old policy.

He replaced the Minister of Trade with Lord Ephlan, and announced the creation of two new regiments, to be permanently stationed in the South and Norwess. This before he buried Rudof. But as for validating war, I know what Powl said. But I also know what he did, whenever push came to shove. And how you saved the king against treachery, and saved Powl from the king."

"He didn't need my help, lad."

"Your reasoning mind tells you to avoid matters of war, Nazhuret, but patriotism is your instinct, deeper than reason."

I recoiled from the duke almost into the fire itself. "Save me from such imputation! Mackim, you bewildered man, does the word 'scientist' mean anything to you?"

The calm certainty faded a little. "I know that you grind glass lenses. It is a metaphor for Vision. And you have studied the meaning of the stars . . ."

I shouted, "The stars have no meaning—save that of their existence. I mapped the stars, long years ago, along with many other people who have not had the misfortune of having their names made public. I make glasses so Grandmother may not replace sugar with salt in the biscuits. I am a scientist who happened to grow up in this cold, backward, and superstitious country, and I do not give you permission to claim me or anything I have done!"

Out of long habit, I had kept my pack in order, so there was nothing for me to do but pick it up and stalk away from his fire. My horse was in the picket line, at one end. She tried to kick me when I approached her with the saddle again, but I didn't take offense.

The young standard-bearer was beside me as I tightened the girth. I don't know how long he had been there. "You are leaving already?"

"Yes. I can't stand it. I'm going to Norwess Palace to throttle Jeram. Or maybe to Vestinglon. I can't believe Benar . . ."

"You're going to end the war?" he asked simply. I had to laugh.

"I don't know what I'm doing, lad. Or what I'm going to do." Seated on the mare, I looked down at his youthful, intelligent face, and I almost asked him to come with me. Had he not made that remark about "the path of the void," I surely would have. Instead I called, "Try to stay alive, son. When my daughter comes, please ask the same of her in my name," and pushed the unwilling mare into the dark.

■   ■   ■

Vestinglon is not far from Norwess: not in terms of the travel I had been doing, but it is cold, jagged, high-altitude going: down to Goss, up again over the old border ridge, and down to the capital. Now that the mare went slowly enough to need pushing, I didn't have the heart to push her.

The air and soil were frozen. All noises rang like bells in the dark. The sky was starless and gray, like a fustian lining to an old coat, but the snow glowed dimly under light from somewhere.

My stomach was hurting, I remember. Want had shrunk it, and I had eaten that evening too much of Velonya's notoriously heavy food. Perhaps I was squirming in the saddle, but the mare began to throw her head in protest, right and left as well as up and down. Her neck was lean and supple, and her head whipped around alarmingly. I lost the reins from numb hands and the mare took off.

I could not see where we were going. I hoped she could. The forest swept by us and over us. I clung to her neck.

I have no clear memory of the branch that swept me off. There was a strong smell in my nose, a confusion and the impact of the frozen ground. I lay there, thinking it unfair that I could not reorder the latest ten seconds of my life: thinking it was too bad. The knowledge that I must freeze in place or catch my horse drove me to my feet again, and I was surprised to see her glimmering on the trail in front of me, only twenty feet away, looking over her shoulder with her damned head and slender neck. I shuffled forward, though all feeling in my feet was gone.

"There you are, you bitch," I said quietly, sniffing through a bleeding nose. "Now don't run away from me. I hate you, but don't run away from me. Only way you'll get your breakfast is from me. You can't reach into your pack, can you?"

She didn't run from me, but neither did she wait. She strode just out of reach, nosing into the brush at either side, ripping icy twigs from the branches. I followed the flicker of her scissoring legs.

I could feel my nose bleeding into the snow. I hoped this would not attract predators. I wondered where the white wolf was that had followed me into the rebels' camp. It seemed irresponsible of me to have lost it. I said as much to the horse, to the wolf, if it was by, and as always, to Arlin.

"Talking to yourself again," she said from the back of the mare.

"No. I'm talking to you," I answered, and sprayed blood in a sneeze.

"Then you should speak up," said my lady.

I followed along, leaning forward so not to stain my clothing. Though I could not feel them, my feet remained under me.

"She's not bad, this mare. Almost like my Sabia, if she were prettier. She certainly goes."

I tried to laugh. "She does that. From Rezhmia's Towers to Bologhini to Cieon across the steppe and all the way up to Norwess. And now this. I don't know why she isn't dead."

I heard Arlin slap the mare's neck in comradely fashion. "I've often wondered that about you, Zhurrie. But some of us are made to endure."

That didn't sound comforting, and I wanted comfort. "Actually, I don't feel very well right now," I said. "My head hurts. My feet are missing altogether."

"I know. But now is what I have, old love, so listen. Do you remember when we first attended the conference of astronomers in Morquenie, over twenty-five years ago? You attended three meetings and one banquet and left, announcing to all and sundry that there was more to science than star charts and more to understanding than could be put in a paper to any society."

This made my head hurt worse. "I remember they were horses' asses. Stuffy, full-of-themselves pedants with obsolete technique and more answers than questions . . ."

"You will get no argument from me, Nazhuret. But I was there to see you, and for a while you acted entirely the creature these poor rebels have tried to make you: mystic, dangerous, exotic . . ."

"I wasn't . . . I'm not . . ." I peered over the horse's white tail, seeing nothing but the dark. "Did you see them all, Arlin? The idiots with the banner? Self-serving Mackim?"

"I saw them and I saw you, love. My cold, practical scientist."

"Cold I am. Very cold. And my stomach hurts. But those people are worse off than any number of pedants. They have perverted Powl's teaching to the point . . ."

"Bullshit. They have no interest in Powl. It is you they follow, Nazhuret, with your half-bred face and your clever hands and words and all the unusual things that have happened around you."

I jogged to keep up. At least it kept me warmer. "Not so unusual. If people would only look about them, life is remarkable."

". . . And if they got the lessons wrong, well—you never condescended to teach them."

I felt this as an injustice. "I never found anyone who would condescend to listen. Except Navvie, and she set up no religious orders. Or do you mean Jeram?"

"At least Jeram tried," said my lady. "And they are astonishing fighters."

We went on for some minutes with no sound but my own labored breathing and the jingling of the horse's pack.

"What are you going to do now?" asked Arlin.

I had been half asleep in my jogging. "Do? I think I'm going to kill the king, love. I think I have to."

There was another few moments of silence. "You could have brought the boy with you," Arlin said, and it took me a while to remember which boy.

"The one who drew the banner? I thought about it. Do you mean I should teach him? If I live through this, I mean? And him. If he lives through this? Do you mean that?"

There was no answer. I sprinted forward, clumsily, finally awakened by my efforts. "You know, Arlin, though I talk to you almost constantly, you're not usually there—out there. I don't usually see you, I mean."

"Do you see me now?" she asked, and I squinted and looked hard at the air above the back of the white horse, but I didn't see Arlin.

Nor hear her more.

I woke in Goss, in a stable, in clean straw and with a pillow under my head. I stared at the oak walls of my stall, and then at the pillow, which was crusty with blood. My head hurt terribly. I heard a banging: maybe my own pulse.

Before I could sit up, or try to do so, a man approached the open door of the stall. He was dressed in a coarse woolen shirt and leather breeches, as befits a groom. "Welcome to the living," he said. "We didn't know whether to feed you or bury you, so we settled on giving you a bed."

I could make no sense out of this, nor out of much else, so he continued, "You walked in here at dawn, behind your horse. She's the one raising dust on the other side of the stable. Doesn't seem to like being stalled."

"I remember the horse, but not this place. Please, where am I?"

"In Goss, where else? Public stable. That hellion of a mare of yours knew where to go, though I don't recall having seen her before. We considered calling a doctor for you, but most of them's off in the war and the ones that's left—well, we decided you'd be better off with horse doctoring. We gave you ice and a cataplasm. Doctor might have drilled a hole in your head to let out the pressure. I seen them do that before."

My good angel squatted down in the straw beside me. It was fairly warm in that place, and yellow straw was heaped over me like a blanket. "I am grateful," I said, and my own voice reverberated unpleasantly in my head. "But why, in a nation ravaged by war, would you waste your time with one stranger?"

He was a middle-aged, middle-weighted man of the usual Velonyan type. His face was as dry as leather, and the stubble of his beard shone gold over it. "Well, maybe it was your mare, bless her nasty heart. She's one of the best I've seen, and from the looks of her, you've gone hard and fast. Mostly, though, I think it was your big dog convinced me you were worth something. I like dogs, and the way this fellow hung by you—his devotion—that convinced me you must be too good to lose."

My head spun, and I wondered if I had lost months of my life to amnesia. Then I remembered and asked, "Is this a long-legged white dog with prick ears and triangular eyes?"

"The very same. I don't know where he is now, but . . ."

"That isn't a dog," I told him. "It is a wolf I killed a few days ago. The mare, too, is a ghost. Thirty years a ghost." I ended that conversation abruptly by passing out.

The next time I woke I was able to stand up, and had a full bladder that made it imperative I do so. In the corner of the stall was my saddle, with packs still attached. Since there was no one in the stable to offend with my distrust, I peeked through the packs and found I had not been robbed of anything, not even money. Perhaps my saintly savior had not even riffled through them. My devoted "dog" was not to be seen, but the mare was pawing, just as she had been doing in her stall at the Towers of Rezhmia City.

Lacking a mirror, I looked at myself in the water trough; my nose was decidedly wider and of a different color. My forehead had an intellectual swelling about it, and also a purple cast. I pulled a bucket and washed the best I could, dressed in clothes in the Velonyan style, put what I could from the mare's pack into mine, left a goodly pile of coins on the straw where I had lain, and set out on foot for Vestinglon.

Before I got to the door of the barn, the whinnies of the mare began to follow me. As I blinked in the sunlight of the doorway, the slams of her body against the stall door also followed me. Before I was well out into the yard, I heard the squeal of steel nails being drawn out and the mare herself followed me. She near knocked me over, getting in front.

"I thought you had enough of this rider," I said to her, and she nodded her head forcefully, but stayed where she was. Despite this unconventional loyalty, it was ten minutes before she allowed me to catch her, and as I felt her limbs for damage she objected to every liberty.

Against all probabilities, the beast seemed sound. I repacked her saddle and lifted it on her, added to the pile of coins in the straw, and once more I mounted. We trotted down the long slope from Goss to the capital no slower than we had left Rezhmia.

My country was still locked in winter, but as we descended the depth of the snow grew less. The ground beneath our feet was mushy, and splashed the belly of the mare and splashed my own legs up to the knees.

There was not so much destruction here, nor refugees to be seen, but there was a strong military presence. Ten miles into our travel I encountered a refectory wagon with a broken axle, dragged by effort into the snowbank at the road's edge. There was an army cook reclining along the driver's hard seat, wrapped in a horse blanket and asleep under the sun. Ahead there seemed to be more vehicles on the road. I took a handy farm driveway and trotted unchallenged down to some decent folks' house and barn, turning from there onto the track the milch cows used in their daily perambulations. The cows had not been turned out today, which was doubtless wise with so many soldiers about, and when their old tracks unwound into a snowy pasture, we continued to the gate, forced it open, closed it behind us, and rode on.

After a half-hour's uncertainty, I found the highway again, and the troops were behind us. We reached Salid by midday, and that meant we were almost to Vestinglon.

Salid is a very old place, which was originally (I have it on authority) a palisaded village in a lake, which could only be reached by boat. Now the town surrounds the lake and the palisade surrounds the gardens that have made Salid famous. They still can only be reached by boat.

I expected to find the place occupied by the army, either Forwall's men or some other general's. I saw no evidence of that: only the white walls, the peaked slate roofs, the calf market, the cabbage stalls, the pubs advertising their summer-brewed and aged ale. All busy, all noisy, not like a nation in civil war. Perhaps the favored status of the place was because so many of the members of our parliament had their houses in Salid instead of Vestinglon proper. But then, Mackim had told me that King Benar had dissolved parliament. I did not sit out in the cold thinking too long about this; I turned into the first public house that possessed a livery, ordered oats, luncheon, and a hot bath. My name there was Tim Glazier.

Unlike Norwess, here no one seemed about to discuss politics, no matter how open I kept my ears.

The mare and I took to the roads for the last stretch of our journey. The sun shone down as brightly as it can in winter's second month. The wind was light and the snow melting. The weather was excellent. It was a fine day to kill my best friend's only son. It was a perfect time to murder my king.

I had dandled this lad on my knee. Only twice, it is true, because his mother did not approve of her husband's raffish friend, and unless Rudof had made a point of it, she kept Benar away from me. At Rudof's request, the boy had received a few lessons horseback from my lady Arlin, but he had called her a few unpleasant names and his father had struck him down from his pony in redhaired rage.

Benar, too, had red hair. As I splashed through the pretty villages and fine fields that surround Vestinglon, I wished heartily that Queen Caudrin had not disliked me so overtly. I had never wished for her affection, for I had none for her. A concealed or polite aversion on both sides would have made no trouble, but the lady was honest, and vocal about it. To Rudof I was always the younger brother he did not otherwise have, and an attack at me brought out the defender in him. Hard on the queen. Harder on Benar.

Crows rose from the side of the road, shining purple in the light. I saw a family of swans waddling over an icy pond. The maples of Vestinglon wove their branches into the sky everywhere. I was almost in tears with the familiar beauty, and with the brilliance of the sun. I entered the bustling city between two wagons: one of onions and one of turnips, their domed tops shining as purple as the crows. Though there were guards wearing the blue and white, they were gaming and I escaped their attention completely.

In Vestinglon there are forty teams of heavy horse that plod the streets all winter, clearing snow with an iron blade. This makes passage easy, but on the other hand it is damned difficult to open one's door after they have passed. I saw the teams, and the red-faced tradesmen with their shovels cursing behind them, and felt such a flow of peace and contentment at being here that I could not myself believe what I had come to do. For the first time in a week, I went into the belly of the wolf, to contain myself. As I did so my demon horse lowered her head, stretched her back, and let out a groaning sigh of relief. I wished I had given her this comfort much earlier.

I did not take Sabia to my favorite stable, but to an overpriced affair that skimped on fodder but was near the palace. I left her there with instructions to quarter-groom her soundly, bran her, and turn her out blanketed into their small paddock. I also warned them that a large dog I had lost might be along anytime. Out of whim I ordered a dinner for it. I pretended I would take my saddle with me, as well as my pack, for I knew the employees here to be thieves, but when no one was looking, I hid both in the hayloft. I left the mare with some doubt I would be able to return for her, if I got out of the palace at all. I hoped she did not look too much like dog food herself.

I cannot describe Vestinglon as I do Canton, or even Rezhmia City, for she is so intimate to me she is like my own round, corn-shock head. I believe her to be more beautiful, however, for all her buildings rise skyward like pikes or good aspirations, and in the winter they outshine the snow.

I must admit that the streets are miserable, because they are old, from the days when little traffic came by coach, but rather by foot of human, ass, or horse. The red bricks of the paving are heaved by frost, however often chained gangs of men hammer them down again.

In Vestinglon there was always the chance I would be recognized, and being dressed in dirt would not make it harder for anyone I knew to pick me out. Easier, perhaps. I had friends among tradesmen, soldiers, scientists and courtiers, beggars and thieves. Of all these, I had only to worry about the soldiers, and though there were many of them in evidence, most seemed to be conscripts, and none of them paid me mind.

On my way to murder the king, I thought I might stop by the Royal Library. I hated to miss a trip to the capital without visiting the stacks. A notion of my own absurdity—to combine regicide with a prowl of the newest publications—sent me into painful giggles, but I stopped at the marble stairs nonetheless.

Before the bronze doors of this establishment is an immense, flat case of glass in which *The Vesting Verity* is posted daily: two copies, really, so both sides of the journal can be read by those who cannot buy the paper themselves. Along with the other men in shabby clothes, I stopped to read. I discovered that the minor uprising of malcontents in the East was nearly all suppressed, and that all of Norwess had established its loyalty to the crown. Foreign influence was suspected in the disturbances. Trials were expected shortly.

When I was eighteen, I had not believed what I read in the newspapers, and the knowledge of my own perspicacity comforted me. Now, at fifty-five, I did not believe what I read in my country's newspapers, and that knowledge made me want to weep.

The journal did not print the usual notice of where the king was that day. That seemed understandable, under a condition of "minor uprising." I hoped the duke was right about his having returned home. I did not go into the library after all.

When Rudof was king, he had spent most of his days at his apartments in the military quarters of the palace. His son had never spent much time there, but now that he was the titular commander of the armed forces, he might have changed his habits. I knew three ways into those apartments that would be unlikely to come to notice. I had shared their secrecy with the king, who liked to get away from things. I also knew a likely servants' entrance into the palace proper, which I learned not from the king but from my lady Arlin, or more exactly, from her old nurse. I did not think I would be able to break and enter both buildings without discovery. I chose the palace as most likely to contain Benar. I figured my chances at one in three.

In the market I bought three things: a cheap shirt, a butcher's apron, and a half of farmed venison. I chose the venison simply because I could not carry a half of beef by myself, and a quarter would not offer enough concealment, but as I blundered along with my face in the aged carcass, I realized I had bought meat that had hung a bit too long, and I felt my disguise to be very appropriate to my errand. People on the street got out of my way. Though it was winter, I heard the buzzing of flies.

I beat on the door with my boot toe. When it was opened by a guard, I said, "Please. I gotta put this down or I'm gonna puke." It was through no deliberate intent that my voice sounded different, but only that I could not make myself breathe through my nose.

The guard grimaced. "Why they want to eat stuff that way I don't know," he said. "Kitchens are to the right."

"I know, I know where they are," I replied, having already turned to the kitchens. Over my shoulder I called, "Maybe if we was nobles, we'd have the taste for it."

But not likely, I added to myself.

There were servants in the joint-kitchen, and despite the midwinter freeze three huge fires burned under the spits. I knew the place well, having once bet on races among the treadmill-dogs that used to power the instruments in the days of my youth. Rudof had won those races easily, for he knew the dogs better than I had. We had baited the long, short-legged hounds with meat scraps taken from an ice closet at the other side of the chamber, which connected with the pastry kitchen. I opened the door and staggered from heat to freezing cold under the weight of the deer. I closed the door behind me, and it was dark. I stumbled over shards of ice, blocks of ice, and frozen carcasses, and despite the cold I could still smell the dead and rotting deer on my clothing. I had a fantasy—almost a hallucination—of the half-frozen, half-rotten bodies of men that must be stacked all over my poor country.

Next my hand slapped something smooth and hard. First I thought it to be leather, but then recognized it as frozen bread dough. When I felt this, I knew where to look for the far door. I had remembered that the doors to the ice closets could always be opened

from within, so as not to freeze some poor scullion solid, and I
hoped such humanity still existed in the king's kitchens. I reversed
my apron, so the smeared meat juice would not be evident, and
opened the door into light.

Before me was a woman with a pig-stomach bladder in her
hand, frosting the latticework on a cake. Between the lines of white
icing were dried cherries, cut in halves. It was enough to make a
man swoon with desire. She looked at me in blank surprise.

"I see the dough is drying out in there," I said with a shade of
ill temper. "How long did you think you could keep it?"

She glanced from me to the door and back. "Master cook, it
isn't my . . ."

"*Isn't your what?*" I shouted. "*Tell* that *to the spoiled bread!*"
She ran to the freezer and I ran from the room.

In the preparation chamber there is a dumb-waiter, used mostly
to bring chocolate to guests in the morning and unpleasant sub-
stances to the sick at all times. Once the king had lowered me in
this contrivance, which had required courage on my part, for Rudof
had a horselike sense of humor and an invincible conviction I could
survive any calamity. Now there was no one to work the thing, but
I managed to push it down past the kitchens enough so I could
climb into the brick chimney which contains it and start to climb.

It was not a difficult stunt, but there was in it so much an air
of our old good times together that I could not keep it in my head
that I was going to murder my dear friend's only son. I kept drifting
from smiles to tears as I humped up my toes and my back alternately
to do the three-story climb.

Up at the fourth floor I found the hatch locked against me, and
for a moment was stymied, but then I remembered the lock was a
simple hook and eye of brass, and though I had left my dowhee
behind, I had a knife. It was not one of my lady's pretty daggers, nor
yet my daughter's scientific throwing knives, but a simple camp
blade with a hinge in the middle and a wooden case. The inelegant
blade slid easily between the hatch and its jamb and popped the
hook.

Getting out was more difficult than climbing, for it required hanging from the jamb for a moment by one hand and one knee, but I did it unobserved, and then I was out on the good carpets of the royal residence. I closed the hatch behind me, resisting the impulse to throw the smelly apron down the chute, where it might be found lying atop the dumb-waiter and give rise to thought. Instead I stuffed it under my shirt, giving myself an imposing belly. At my age, I deserved one.

Most of the rooms along this hall were the use-rooms of the queen's ladies. There was also a library, which Rudof had made his own. Most of the books in it were rare and precious (at least to a person like myself) and at least half were not in Velonyie. I had never seen his son there, even to visit, and did not imagine many of the palace accessories had an interest in science or foreign histories. I determined to wait in this room behind a certain couch I knew, and use my senses to help me locate the king, if he was here.

I heard nothing in the corridor, and nothing from any door along the hall. I slipped to the third door along the right, opened it, and went in.

There was the room, just as I had left it four years before. There, against the far wall, was the leather settee. Sitting upon it, a large volume open upon his lap, staring up at me startled, was young King Benar.

My body left my mind far behind, leaping the distance from door to settee. My weight struck Benar in the chest, and we both went over, hitting the carpet and rolling once. My body did not finish the work, however, and I was left with the young monarch straining away from me, my hand over his mouth and my own mouth spitting out strands of his auburn hair.

I wedged my left knee into the small of his back, and with some difficulty I forced him onto his stomach and pulled his head back from the carpet. In this position he was open to a rabbit punch, which would break his neck cleanly. I did not deliver that punch. I sat there for some moments, riding the king of Velonya like a jockey on a horse, but I did not strike him.

He was trying to speak—not scream or shout, but speak—and I slipped my hand up to his nose.

"Is this . . . did you come to steal me away?" he asked, his voice twisted by the stretch upon his throat. "Like my father and you planned for the sanaur, when you ended the Summer War?"

"I came to kill you, to end the Winter War," I answered, and my own voice was not much more pleasant.

This seemed to catch him by surprise. His body bucked under me once, and then he went limp. "Then do it and be over," he whispered.

I let my knees slip sideways, until I was straddling him. I listened in the corridor, but there was no sound. I remember the smell of dust and dirty wool from the carpet. "For the last twenty-five years you have considered me your enemy, Benar. Now that you have made me your enemy in truth, why shouldn't I kill you?" I heard myself justifying my actions, and closed my mouth.

Benar took a deep breath, which rocked me back and forth. I kept my free hand between his shoulder blades, with my weight behind it. He was lithe and well built, but not his father's equal in size. Nor had he been taught by his father's teacher, or by his father. Nor me.

"You were not King Rudof's enemy, so how can you be entirely mine, Nazhuret? At least that is what I thought . . ."

"It is because I was not your father's enemy that I have come to kill you."

I could feel him testing himself under me, but nothing gained him purchase. When my words did not seem to be followed by action, he sighed. "This is unbearable. Why don't you do it?" And in another mood, "Are they really thinking . . . saying . . . that I killed my father?"

"A goodly number of 'they' are," I said, and I chuckled. It was a grim, inadequate laugh, but having let it loose, I was aware that I had lost my last chance to kill the king. My mind was in utter refusal, and even my hands let him go. "Did you?"

"Oh, my God!" said Benar. As I rolled off him, he turned on his side, curled like a hedgehog, and hid his face behind one hand. I pulled that hand away. "Did you?" I asked again.

He said, "No," and he said it with no elaboration. He did not try to get up.

"Did your mother?"

At this his warm brown eyes narrowed in his narrow, half-Lowcantoner face. "For three years before his death, my mother had not been in the same city as her husband."

That I had known. "Still, did she kill him?"

He rolled over on his back, releasing the full mustiness of the carpet. "I am not in any position to know," he said to me. "You would know that better than I. Anyone might know that better than I." He sneezed. I remembered he had had asthma, as a boy. "All my advisers told me I wasn't suspected in Papa's death."

He looked full and intent at me. "It is supposed to be some scorned mistress. He had many . . . paramours. You knew that, of course."

"Yes and no." Since I had lost my chance at murder, I straightened up and righted the settee again. I sat down upon it. It smelled better than the carpet. "We never spoke of it. He probably knew I would be . . . judgmental about the matter."

The king of Velonya made to sit beside me and then thought better of it. "And yet you lived with . . . you lived unmarried for so many years with the Lady Charlan Bannering."

His entry into my own private history offended me, but I considered that this man, being king, had no privacy himself and I reined myself in. "Arlin and I could not marry, because I was dispossessed and dared not have legitimate offspring. Nobles are jealous of their possessions, whether old or newfound."

I don't know if Benar had been given that explanation for the long, central scandal of my life. He was enough a king that I could not read it in his face. He merely nodded. "Nobles are also ambitious for new possessions. Is this not the real explanation for the rebellion in Norwess?"

I gazed at his wary, expressionless face and felt a strong desire to spank the king. I could not think what good that would serve, so instead I answered, "Nobles are ambitious, certainly, but had Rudof died by falling off his horse, I think there would be no war today.

"Listen to me, Benar. Perhaps I am also ambitious. My aunt in Rezhmia has promised to recognize me as rightful king of Velonya. The connection with your line is tenuous, but with enough regiments in occupation—Rezhmian regiments—it will become more convincing. You see, the Rezhmians cannot afford to have a clear enemy on their northwestern border. They intend to take Velonya out while it is at war with itself . . ."

"A war they themselves have financed and fomented!"

"No!" I shouted. "No. Wait until you see what sort of war the sanaur'l *could* finance and . . . and foment, if she desires. What you have is Velonyan outrage, and most ironically, it is outrage at foreign intervention.

"Benar, a large percentage of Velonya wishes your mother and her whole tribe to hell. Get used to it. Deal with that or you cannot deal as king of Velonya."

Anger had overcome Benar's wariness, and he sat himself on the settee with me and pointed a finger. "First you tell me you're going to be king of Velonya and then you dare to lecture me on top of it."

I slapped the finger away. "I don't *want* to be king. I loathe the prospect. At my age, too! But I look at you and I don't think you're big enough to save me from it!"

"Look who is talking about 'big'!" shouted the young king, and then the door opened and Count Dinaos stepped in. We both stared.

"Forgive the interruption, sir. That geography you recommended. You said it was here . . . ?"

King Benar had been reading from a book of maps, which now lay spine-spread against a bookcase with its pages like crushed feathers beneath it. Without will, the king stared toward the book, which Dinaos retrieved. Leaning against the case, he smoothed the abused paper, page by page.

"How are you here?" I asked. I found my hands were folded in my lap. I was blinking.

"By packet, of course," he said. "Much faster that way. And of course, more civilized than riding the roads."

I cleared my throat, which had grown slightly hoarse. "And your shoulder?"

He rolled it tentatively. "Not perfect. But it is better every day, thanks to you and the doctor."

"I don't know about this," said the king, looking from one of us to the other. The spell of good manners had somehow taken control of the situation, and he seemed as disinclined to continue shouting as I was. "Are you acquainted with my mother's cousin, Nazhuret?"

I, in my turn, stared at Dinaos. "Not with your mother's cousin, exactly, sir. With a fellow traveler on a boat, who does most excellent oils, yes."

"You flatter me, Nazhuret," Dinaos said, not meaning it. He closed the book. "We never traded genealogies. Why should we have?" He smiled smoothly, bowed to us both, and opened the door.

"I will be in my room," he said, and then he closed the door behind him.

For a moment it was very quiet. Dust still hung in the air from our squabble. I thought about the situation, as though I had never thought about it before. "Do you want to end the war?" I asked Benar.

What started on the young face as a smile ended as exposed teeth. "I did not start the war, and it is not the king who can conclude it. The king is not the government; you know that. My father saw to stripping himself of his own power. Parliament . . ."

"I am told you have dissolved parliament."

He scowled. "No. No one has presumed to dissolve parliament. It recessed for thirty days around Yule, but it is in session beginning next week."

"Then next week you can tell parliament you will mediate. The king is not the government, but the king's murder began this and the king's intervention is the best way I know to stop it."

Though his face was no longer masked, the emotions that flew over it were too fleeting for me to recognize. At last it soured. "The generals will not let me. Already they 'protect' me into the state of a prisoner, and if I challenge the government I expect I will be 'protected' into legal guardianship."

I did not ask whether the young man expected his mother would be part of that destructive protection. It no longer made any difference. "Then," I said to him, "I guess I must steal you away, as your father and I planned to do to the sanaur of Rezhmia during the Summer War."

"But there is the problem, man! To where? If I knew what generals might follow me, then I would have stolen myself, weeks since."

"To Norwess, my king. To the rebels."

Benar slammed the little couch so hard he almost tipped us again. "The rebels? Certainly—there's the very army to take my orders! I'd exchange this close watch for the end of a common thief's rope! I was a fool to trust you."

I let the young king rage and I let him pace, because I could not deny the possibility he might end—not at the end of a rope, for the rebels had more respect for royalty than that—but at the headsman's ax. He paced exactly like his father, though his legs were not so long.

"Nonetheless, Benar, it seems you do trust me. Which I find disturbing. I did come to kill you, and I am usually simple enough to do what I set out to do. But if you go with me it will not be as prisoner, I assure you, and if the rebels will not parlay with you respectfully, then you will not face them alone."

He stopped still and glared at me, and he was such a perfect stranger to me and was yet so much his father that all my hair stood on end. "You and who else will be with me?"

I had a ridiculous idea. "Let's find out," I said, and I opened the door out of the library. King Benar of Velonya followed on my heels.

"Where is Dinaos's room, sir?" I whispered.

"My mother's cousin is quartered down this very hall," replied Benar in even quieter tones. "Behind the gilt-crest door. He has but one servant with him, a dumb man, and if we are reasonably quiet . . ."

I ran down the carpeted hall and knocked at the ornate door. The pirate opened it almost instantly. "I'm glad to see you survived the Felonks," I said to him. "Not to mention the sea serpent. And the ocean."

He gave me no smile at all, but bowed himself away, and Dinaos was there, his finger closed into his place in the book. He invited us both in, bowing lightly to the king.

"I wondered," I said, "whether you'd like to help us do something interesting."

The king let out an audible gasp. I thought he might stalk out of the room and down the hall at that moment, either to get the guard or to return to the library and forget I had happened.

"Interesting in what sense, Nazhuret? Politically interesting, or in an artistic sense? If you mean anything more personal than these, I do not suggest we involve my nephew, even though he be handsome, dashing, and highest in the land."

If King Benar gasped again, I did not hear it.

I wanted to answer Dinaos in the same vein of wit, as Powl might have answered, or even my lady Arlin. But I cannot fence with words; in this I am the typical, stolid Velonyan. "I want to escort His Majesty to the Great Square—no, rather to the Tuesday Market. There is still a Tuesday Market, isn't there? He wishes to address his people directly."

Benar grabbed my arm. "And are you telling me what I am to say to my people? Directly?"

"No, sir, I do not presume. I merely aspire to get you there."

Dinaos did not touch me, but I was far more aware of his physical presence in front of me than I was of the grip of the young king. "To escort the king of Velonya is always, of course, a great honor." He searched around for a bookmark and at last took the hand of his servant and placed it firmly between the pages. "I must change, but that won't be a moment. Then I will request three horses suitable for hunting—for me, my man, and to pack game. I regret I will not have the entertainment of accompanying His Majesty and yourself out the window because of this tedious shoulder of mine, but I have no doubts you will be able to find us."

He turned to the mute pirate, who still stood with his hand pressed firmly between the pages of the geography. "Out the window, Sieben. I said they are going out the window."

The man was quick about finding the bookmark his master had left lying beneath a cup, and he disappeared through the door. Dinaos strolled into his 'tiring room, and King Benar sat down heavily at the table. "Why do you trust him?"

"I . . . He is his own . . ." I was very bad at words today. I almost said, "I am close to him," but I was not sure what I meant by that, so I only sighed and nodded to the king.

Sieben returned with a long hemp rope, with overhand knots measured along its length, like a fathoming rope from a vessel. "Where on the good earth did you find that so quickly?" asked King Benar.

I, who had grown up a servant, only thanked him and tried to take it from him. With a black look, Sieben held it back from me, knotted the end soundly around one leg of a massive armoire, and opened the window to the winter freeze. Slowly, he lowered it down.

"He's a pi—a sailor," I said to the king. "The knot will hold. Can you descend?"

The young king snorted. "I'm not a girl," he said, and then his eyes shifted in embarrassment from the door where Dinaos busied himself in the 'tiring room to myself and back to the rope.

I thought it only polite in an endeavor of this sort to go first, so I leaned out the window and found myself overlooking a drab, frozen yard of flagstone. I swung over and went down fast, both to keep my hands from going numb on the rope, and because even in midwinter Velonya, people do sometimes look out their windows.

I worried as Benar crawled out after me. As he had said, he was "not a girl" and was young besides, but rope climbing is a specialized skill, not practiced by kings. Then I laughed at myself, thinking how not an hour ago I had been intent upon the same man's death. He came down sprightly enough, and was holding something tightly in his teeth.

I gave him my hair-stuffed Sekret overcoat, which became a

jacket of waist length and three-quarter sleeves upon the king. It smelled no better on royalty. The thing he had been carrying was Dinaos's Lowcantoner dress hat, and Benar looked a sight wearing it atop the barbaric jacket. I myself was too nervous to feel the cold.

All I had for disguise was the kerchief in my pocket, and I didn't think it wise to try for the appearance of a Rezhmian. I followed along in the king's wake as I used to follow in that of his father, feeling as uneasy about things as I had in years before.

"It will take him time to get the horses," I said into King Benar's ear.

"If he gets them," he answered me. "I don't have your reasons to trust the man."

"What do you mean, my reasons? He's family to you: not to me. And if you don't trust him, sir, why are you doing this?"

Benar gave me a cool glance. "If he fails me, it's up to you to find a way out. And as for your reasons, Nazhuret of Sordaling, I do not presume to discuss them. But all the capital knows the tastes of my uncle Count Dinaos, and you are no stranger here, either."

Many times in my life I had been mistaken for a sexual invert because of my lady's fondness for men's clothing. I had always known the facts, taken the mistake as a great joke, and kept my peace about it. Now I was not sure what the truth was, but I still kept my peace about it.

"We'll go to the stables," said the king. "That's the easiest way to meet him, or if he does not arrive, we can get horses on our own."

There was a bitter wind, and that odd-shaped and rambling building had sliced it narrowly, so that as we moved it struck at us from different angles. My eyes watered, so I was forced to walk with my head down, which was clumsy and unobservant. My consolation was that every other soul in the yards had his head down, too. Benar kept both hands to his ridiculous hat, which still snapped in the wind.

He scraped close to the side of an ell and I hurried to follow, when I seemed to blunder into a patch of light. My teary eyes dazzled and I wiped them, trying to make out the figure before me.

It was dressed in homespun and leggings, with blond hair illumi-
nated by its own private sun. I recognized the boy—the maker of
the wolf banner.

"Your daughter is safe with us," he said. "She arrived this
morning." He stepped back two paces and faded.

Benar came into focus just beyond that spot. He was glaring at
me. His hat was still popping in the wind. I did not know what to
say; I feared if I mentioned the event I might be convicted of
insanity. I pretended the wind had blown something in my eye.

"Who the hell was that?" asked the young king. He strode
through the spot the messenger had vacated, stamping the ground
as if to raise the phantom by force. "You did see him, didn't you?"

"Of course, sir. I met him in Norwess. In the flesh, that is. I
don't remember his name: only that he was on the third level. Of
the void, I think."

Benar slunk close to the bricks of the wall, holding his hat
brim so close to his chin he seemed to want to tie it there. "And
what does all that mean? Something to do with the 'belly of the
wolf'?"

I shrugged.

"Why do you claim ignorance of this? I thought all those idiots
were imitating Nazhuret of Sordaling."

"So did Nazhuret. It shows you how wrong we can be, doesn't
it?" I pressed him to walk on, into the wind again. "He came to tell
me that my daughter was safe."

"I'm glad to hear that—my regards to her," the king bellowed
politely against the blowing. "Had you been worried?"

"Oddly enough, no. I've been too busy to worry much, and I
have certainly had no premonitions of disaster. Which makes it a
very strange visitation, doesn't it? Lacking in drama."

"Oh, I don't think so," Benar said, "but the visitations I am
used to are of state, and tend to be slow and long-winded."

"This one was certainly not long-winded," I answered.

When we were beside the commercial gate, he shouted again.
"This lad—the void fellow. Is he amongst us? I mean, is he alive or
dead?"

"Alive when I last saw him, sir."

"And he didn't mention any recent change of state?"

I shook my head. "Just the single message. That's all."

■ ■ ■

The count met us as we drew near the stable. He was standing beside three solid-looking horses, richly geared. Only two of them bore riding saddles, and I wondered who amongst us he intended to jam into the pack saddle like a dead deer. Dinaos adjusted very fussily a girth that the groom had already perfectly adjusted. He did not look up at our approach, but said, "My man will ride and lead the third horse until we are out of sight of this place, and then it will be the work of a moment for him to steal a more appropriate caparison. Then he will walk behind in case we need other services."

The king gave an interested glance toward Dinaos's mute pirate. "Good at a number of things, is he?" The pirate did not return the glance.

"Any number." The count mounted and started forward, his face blandly set into its usual self-approval. The pirate followed, and so did the pack horse, the king of Velonya, and I. "I already have a horse and saddle, my lord," I called forward. "North in the city."

He leaned over and frowned at me thoughtfully. "Not that beast I put under you in Ighelun?"

He was teasing me, but it was the sort of game guaranteed to make a poor man blush. I explained with what dignity I had that his horse was left in my aunt's care until I could retrieve it. He gave a grunt and one eyebrow rose. "Well, as long as the good woman has fodder enough for it, I don't mind."

I assured the count that my aunt did. I also gave it as my opinion that we would do better with me afoot in the market, as well as the pirate Sieben. The king gave me a moment's worried look, but made no objection. He mounted the other ready horse and we went forward at a good rate, with myself trotting in the lead and the pirate behind.

I am not such a fool as to claim the king was not recognized. As our odd party pushed through the crowds of Crown Quarter, I doubt a minute passed when I did not catch someone staring, sometimes with dropped jaw, at the spectacle of their own monarch wrapped in barbarian quilting, one hand pressing a very floppy antique hat to his head. But no one spoke, and especially none spoke to us, for all believed that the king of Velonya could dress as he wished and move where he wished.

It seemed pure bad fortune when we crossed the Vesting Canal bridge and found a small troop of blue-and-white dragoons blocking the road leading left to Court Market Square. They were engaged in warming themselves trooper-style, with a cup of hot mull in the hand and a warm horse under the seat-bones. I heard one man make a joke about the effect the cold was having on his balls, and judged by the quality of their laughter that they had been balancing their cups for a while now. I started to wave my party back, thinking to move left at the next block, but Count Dinaos pushed his mount past me.

"Soldiers, your king!" he shouted, the sharp consonants of Lowcanton making the words yet more aggressive. I heard more than one cup hit the cobbles. Benar cursed under his breath, but he took off his silly hat. The two nobles rode through the confusion, and before they reached the end of the block, the troopers had swung their horses into a good imitation of military attention.

The king pulled in his own horse and looked at them. I stood in front and looked also. One uniform had its white frontlet stained with wine, like a great red heart wound. That man was breathing hard, and I wondered how hot the wine had been. Another was still struggling to find his sword hilt under his huge dragoon cloak, but all had their eyes fixed on the king, and what the king saw in those eyes must have been encouraging, for he spoke.

"Dragoons, attend me, if you please. To the market."

His voice in command was less harsh than that of Count Dinaos, but no less effective. The dozen men swung neatly into double file at the sides of the king and count, four leading, six following, and one to either hand. They boxed in the pirate and me, and made us watch our feet.

I could see nothing but horse legs and horse hinds, but I knew the area well enough to know when we had debouched into the market square. Here the crowd brought the horses almost to a halt. One of the dragoons brought out a small cornet and blew it to clear a path. We were not doing very well with our attempt at secrecy.

I heard Benar give a shout, and he pointed. "Kinnett! Damn my luck! It's Colonel Kinnett, the adjutant. He's seen us, and there he goes, on foot, the bastard!"

I found my prison of horse bodies intolerable, and in desperation I threw myself upon the pack saddle and balanced standing atop the spare horse's back. "One of you men, fetch him for the king," I bellowed. "King Benar wishes to speak with the colonel."

The dragoon with the cornet shot me a glance that went from questioning to delighted, and I recalled the rivalry between cavalry and headquarters staff that exists in every army of the civilized world. He shot away, honking his horn merrily, and I doubted the colonel adjutant would get very far.

The king turned and looked up at me on my acrobatic perch. "Shall I incorporate every man I find dangerous to me into this little company, Nazhuret?"

"It seems to be working, sir," I said, and I slid down onto the lashings of the saddle. It spread my legs very wide, and as the pirate led me forward, I felt more and more childlike and not like a man of fifty-five at all. I believe I laughed.

The king stood on the granite base of his grandfather's war memorial (the war against Rezhmia that was lost, and the war that was responsible for my own being), and I am trying to remember what he said to the market crowd that morning. The words seemed very stirring at the time. He said Velonya was one people and had always been one people, and though that is a falsehood, it is a comfortable one, even to a man like me who is not one people in himself. He said further, and this I believe true, that a broken nation would soon be gobbled up by foreign potentates. With the cunning of his long training, he refrained from naming the potentates and so offended none of the wives and burghers listening. Then he said he was going that very day to the camp of the rebels in Norwess to discuss their grievances and mediate the peace.

There was a stout lady next to me, carrying a wicker basket half as large as she was. This she dropped under my horse, which tried to dance away from it, while the lady wailed, "Ah, the little one will be murdered!" It took me a moment to realize she was talking about the king. I told her he had a better chance of losing his head to his own generals than to the rebels, but I did not tell her his odds were short in either case.

Before King Benar was done, I heard a shouting from the crowd, and standing again I saw the mass pressed and cut by a phalanx of soldiery in blue and white. "Dragoons!" I shouted. "Protect your king!"

I need not have bothered. The horsemen cut through the crowd, and I saw one old woman go down screaming under hooves. I slid down from my perch to find her, and then was in peril from the close-ridden horses myself. I fended off the big beasts on both sides with my elbows, but was unable to find the poor woman; I can only hope some citizen pulled her from the cobbles. Now I had to use those same elbows against the populace, which closed behind the cavalry like water behind a ship. The water was roaring.

There came an order from the sergeant of dragoons, and his men surged forward. In order to prevent losing them entirely, I had to grab a horse's tail and be dragged. It was God's mercy I was not kicked in the head. "Where is the king?" I shouted to the rider, and he saw me there, attached to his mount in this ignoble manner, and he slashed me across the face with his steel-weighted crop, opening the skin under one eye and across the bridge of my nose. The sting of it was terrible, and I smelled and tasted blood again.

"I'm sorry, boy. I did not recognize you as the king's man," the dragoon said calmly, but I was not calm. I don't believe I was even human as I leaped to grab the man's saddle cantle, hauled myself up behind the dragoon, and took the man by his collar and sash and hauled him above my head and into the air. He landed on the pavement badly, and I took his saddle.

There in the midst of the dragoons rode the king, astride but still seeking his stirrups. The blades of his bodyguard flashed in the sun and the surrounding infantry did not yet challenge them.

Though I could not reach my own stirrups by a good four inches, I kicked the horse forward and he shoved his body next to King Benar's horse.

The king was flushed: with anger or the euphoria of battle I could not tell. He looked at my bloody face and scowled. "Damn you, Nazhuret Eydlson; what have you gotten me into? They will kill me and it will be for nothing at all."

At that moment I wished I had succeeded in killing the brat earlier, regardless what became of Velonya. That this pouting politician should be the son of his gallant father seemed impossible. It occurred to me that were it not for the red hair, I could kill Benar now, here in the square. I answered him nothing at all, but drove my stolen horse to the front of the wedge and bellowed to be heard above the noise of the crowd.

"Citizens of Velonya! Stand by your king! Not the blue and white, but the king! The king! The king!"

A musket ball sang by my ear, and as though that was a signal, the crowd took up my chant. I felt another leg nudge mine as a horse was pressed close.

Dinaos had either doffed his hat or lost it. He, too, scowled at me, but meditatively. "You don't even like my nephew, Nazhuret. Why take his insults, instead of his crown?"

I had to spit blood from my lips in order to answer. "Because I love Velonya, my lord. And I am not Velonyan enough to stand as its king. I am what I am." I had to spit again.

"What you are is scarred, my dear savage. Unless you have that quickly tended. Such a shame: a slave's wound. I presume you killed the man?"

I told Dinaos to let it be. That I might well not have to worry about scars in the future, nor did I care about the quality of the damage, save that it stung.

The battle was not between armed horsemen and infantry; it was between infantry and the mass of unarmed flesh, as the citizens who stood yards away angrily shoved the bodies of the citizens who stood closer onto the blades of the regulars. I heard a woman shriek, "My babies! Let us out of here!" and I felt perfectly how I had

caused this situation: this carnage. I grabbed for the king's horse's
bridle, to pull him forward. At the moment I was more concerned
with getting his dangerous presence away from the unarmed mar-
keters than I was with saving him from capture, but no matter—I
missed the catch anyway.

Benar was going fast, even without my help. He clung to the
neck of his horse, which was a courtly beast and not battle hard-
ened at all. It hopped and kicked at each report of powder, but that
same fear made the horse plunge through the crowd, which a fine
hack like that one surely would not otherwise have done.

My own cavalry mount had no compunctions about trampling
things. We went over what had been a fish barrow, and my nose
was hit by the stink of smashed trout as well as human blood. The
cold had already closed off the bleeding of my face. Both the king's
horse and mine were caught briefly in the torn canvas of a stall, and
brassware rolled and clanged around us, and then I could see the
other side of the square, where the shops we call "red brick palaces"
stood in glassy rows, with the shop owners' establishments above
them. For a moment I saw myself in what I thought was a broken
window, but then I recognized the diagonal break as being on my
face instead of in the glass. Once past a florist, with its winter
display of hellebore and straw bouquets, and we were on Grand
Avenue, where to my relief and amazement the thoroughfare was
not being held against us. The king was on his way.

Battle was still behind us, and the intersection was corked by
the people we had swept along, either by force or by enthusiasm. I
felt a tentative tapping on my ankle and looked down to see Sieben,
looking no worse for his passage. He motioned that he would come
up behind me, and that and our location gave me an idea. I swung
down from the horse.

"Take it. I'll be back in five minutes."

I tried to say the same to Dinaos or the king, but the whip-
slash made it impossible for me to screw up my face enough to
shout. I ran between horses and off the avenue, where one block
away stood the stable where I had left Sabia.

The stablehands were all out, probably gaping at the melee

in the square. I found the mare chewing the door of her stall; she had done a bit of damage already. In the cleaning room I also found alcohol and ointment for saddle sores. I splashed both over my face and screamed at the result. I had the gray mare saddled within two minutes and rode her out. There was no one to take my money.

The king's dragoons were not where I had left them. Taking advantage of the open road, they were galloping over the flagstones. The mare from Rezhmia, having just this day finished a week of abusive work, took their flight as a challenge. She caught up with them within sixty seconds.

The rear guard spun around to face me with sabers raised before they recognized my face—or at least recognized the slash across it. I was permitted to pass up between their ordered line to the king.

"So you didn't run," he said.

I found I could not use my face for expression, and could only speak in a mumble. "You didn't think I had," I said.

Count Dinaos was still by Benar's side, riding as for a jolly hunt. He glanced at me, winced sympathetically, and then his attention was caught by the mare. His black eyes first shone with surprise and then avidity. "I thought she was dead," he whispered. "Dead these twenty-five years. Or is this her daughter?"

The gaunt mare was dancing between the horses of the king and the count, seeming to disdain them. "I don't know who or what she is, my lord," I told him. "I call her Sabia, and she can outgo anything without wings."

He nodded. "And what do you call the dog?"

I did not look down, though I felt the same sweat come over me as I had each time the inexplicable animal had appeared. I thought of a dozen cowardly explanations, and almost said the white dog was from the livery where I had kept the mare and would doubtless return home after a block or so. What I did say was "I have no dog," and Dinaos did not pursue the subject.

That afternoon's action is now called in histories "The Battle of Tuesday Market" by some, and in other places, "The Battle for

Kingly Loyalty." If I had to pick between the two, I like the "Market" title better, because I instigated the damned thing, and I had no loyalty to the king at all. But I'd rather name it "The Battle of Bloody Cobbles" or, better yet, "The Battle of Armed versus Unarmed." At the time, we were aware of blood and slaughter, but would not have called it a battle.

What happened during that long afternoon as we rode from the city is harder yet to explain. I ask the reader, if despite me there comes a reader, to reflect upon human nature and human habit, and perhaps he or she will understand. I admit I don't.

We left the city as a small troop of cavalry surrounding the king, accompanied by burghers and peasants on foot, and all of us assailed periodically by three brigades of infantry: Gorham's first, fourth, and eighth regiments, The King's Own, and the much smaller City Zouaves, to whom Colonel Kinnett was attached. Their form of assault was to press heavily against the dragoons, using nothing but their bayonet points lightly against the flanks of the horses, to get close enough to influence the king. With the peasantry the soldiers were not so considerate.

We were in the river suburb, where as a child I had saved my pennies to ride the swanboats with my ragamuffin-love Charlan, when a great roar of enthusiasm rang through the dragoons, and at least two thousand horsemen swept through infantry and peasantry alike and joined with our little bodyguard. I did not know whether this was catastrophe or rescue, and I believe neither did the king, but they made around the royal person a ring of protection much larger than before, and the blue and white was fluttering at our head.

"We have a chance," shouted Benar into my ear. "I didn't believe it until now, but we have a chance." Then he added, "I have to piss. I have had to since we left the square. How can I stop all these?"

I said, "You can't. You don't, sir. You lean over one stirrup, unbutton, and try not to dirty your own horse. Nor my leg, if you please."

As he continued to stare at me, I nodded my head forcefully.

"That is how it is done. Among the Naiish they even . . . well, no matter. No one will see but me."

I was inaccurate in that, for Count Dinaos noticed and he laughed in the rudest fashion. But he is the king's uncle.

Before the early dusk of winter we received a letter, passed from horseman to horseman, that General Degump of the Zouaves wished the king to understand that his allegiance in this matter was not at all in question; they were all king's men. Benar showed this missive to Dinaos and myself. "How can I ever trust the man?" he asked.

It was Count Dinaos who answered, his mouth as bright with teeth as any shark's. "You don't trust him, Bennie. You use him. Put his men between your cavalry and the rest, where they will be first hit if there is a strike against you. See if they obey."

The Zouaves did obey, and I watched their blousy, brilliant uniforms and their black horses make a border around our strange assemblage.

The speed at which a mass of soldiery can move seems to be inverse to its number, and my mare rested as she carried me. By dark—and marching men call it dark earlier than do riders—the crimson wagons of the City Zouaves had forced themselves forward to meet the king, filled with the finest of fine gear for winter camping. As it turned out, Benar commandeered an estate on the banks of the Velon River, and it was the Zouaves themselves who camped in the snow around it, making a circle of bright campfires around the bright windows of the mansion.

I got to dine with the king and bunk with him as well, and I do not know whether this was from royal favor, or to make certain I was subject to the maximum risk.

By now the cold had numbed my twice-damaged nose, but there were military doctors to see to the wound, and but for the interference of Count Dinaos I might have been subject to them, and perhaps had my nose amputated. Sieben the pirate stitched it up with fine silk thread he raided from the ladies' chambers, and he used very small stitches, each of which hurt.

"You may be presentable after all," said the count, who

watched all while swishing brandy in a blown snifter. "But if you are not, at least we will still have the painting. I am glad of that."

The pain of the needle brought tears to my eyes, and I was surprised to hear his voice very close in my ear. "It was you, wasn't it, who thought to bring me along on this promenade? Not my nephew, but you?"

I admitted as much.

"Why?" he asked, and I could feel his breath in my right ear, and smell the fine old brandy he was holding to my lips. Blinking, I whispered that I didn't know why, and he held the glass up for me to drink, and took it away again and kissed me. Through fumes and tears I could not see him at all.

"Not that I feel that you owe me for the deed, Nazhuret. I am immensely amused by everything today except your Velonyan weather."

I wiped my eyes on my sleeve and then I could see him again, swirling his brandy, looking more bored than amused, and not at all like a man who had just kissed another man on the lips.

"One by one," he said, in the same languid tone, "your regimental and brigade commanders are coming to visit the king, explaining that any conflict was a hideous misunderstanding. The problem now will be to explain this crowd to your rebels as a mediation for peace."

"And the people? The commoners who followed us? Now that it's cold and we're . . ." I found it almost impossible to talk with the new stitches.

Dinaos shrugged, and this gesture was freakishly like one of Arlin's shrugs. I took the brandy from his hand without invitation and downed the glass. He looked less bored and more amused. "The peasants are gone, to wherever peasants go at night. Like birds, I suppose, they have their nests. Perhaps they will accompany us again tomorrow, if we strew crumbs of rhetoric."

I rose from the stool where Sieben had placed me, and it was in my mind to tread out into the snow and go "wherever the peasants go." It seemed that there, finally, was my loyalty, and if their use in this expedition led to death by freezing, then I ought to freeze with them. I found my head a bit light, however, and my vision a bit speckled. The pirate took me by both shoulders.

"Oh, and your dog is being warmed in the kitchen," said Dinaos, still calmly. "Though if that is a dog, I am an Ighelun fisherman."

We were in one of the smaller dining rooms, where the rug had been rolled up to prevent the spatter of my blood in this surgery. I had forgotten the animal, but as Dinaos spoke I became aware of it, I don't know how, and I pointed to the place from where I felt it. "There?"

The count nodded. "Yes. The dragoons had a hard time with it, but it is locked away now."

"It—attacked them?"

He made a face. "No, no, Nazhuret. It whined and wiggled and squirmed to be with you. They might have let it in out of compassion, but I said no, lest it joggle my man's hand."

I saw the terrible creature in my mind's eye, sliced open in the snow, and then rollicking, unharmed, behind me. "Tell me, my friend. This dog. Is its coat somewhat . . . pink?"

"Pink? Oh, yes, I see what you mean. Yes, it bears all its wounds. What have you done to it?"

Now I could stand without help. "I killed it." I stepped in the direction of a white wooden door, and I felt strong enough to make the little journey to the kitchen.

"And now you must kill it again?" he asked lightly. Sieben just stood there, one hand holding a bloody needle.

"No," I answered. "I don't think so. Not anymore."

Behind the white door was an oven room, now cold, and behind it another door, this with a chair propped against it. I removed the chair and stepped into the lightless kitchen.

I could hear it; a scraping over the tiles and a whine. There were two windows and only the light of campfires far below. "What this time?" I whispered to the wolf. "Do you try to kill me or do I try to kill you? Do you follow or . . . or do you lead?"

Its nails clicked over the floor in a path that hugged the walls. It seemed about as eager to come to me as any wild beast is when locked in a room with man. "They said you loved me, you . . . thing. Or at least were firmly attached to me. Maybe the latter is more true. Maybe you like it as little as I do. Maybe you, too, have no choice in the matter."

Now I could see the pale form, so tall, so long, like a caricature of a starved dog. Its head was almost on the tiles, and its tail between its hind legs. It sought to hide under the iron stove, but I could still see it, and it knew.

I was suddenly as weary as I deserved to be, and I sat down on the cold kitchen floor. I stopped looking at the wolf. "Once, we might have been very simple friends, you and I. I shared my food with you, but you wouldn't share yours with me. Remember?

"You took up with the werewolf. Or were you the werewolf? I ask you, was there a werewolf at all, or only a sick man?" I glanced up, and the wolf had crawled half out from under the stove, and its eyes shone at me green as beech leaves. I couldn't bear that beauty, so I looked at my worn old hands instead.

"Every time I have seen a ghost, and that is about every time I have killed a man, I have seen you, too. Yet I hadn't killed you then. Only tossed a stone at you. In fact, weren't you the ghost of the first man I killed? I thought so once.

"Since then, I admit I have killed you. It was legitimate, for you were trying to kill me, or my horse. Weren't you?"

I looked up again and the eyes were very close to me. Green as jade. "Are you death, Whitey? My own private death, which has never found me, but which I am so good at inflicting upon others?

"How do I come to have a white death that follows me? How do I come to create a banner for other men—to *be* a banner for men I cannot understand and who cannot understand me?" My eyes were filling with tears.

"Whitey, I wish I had stayed a servant at Sordaling School all the days of my life. I wish with all my heart I had died with Arlin. I wish I could die now, and let all the world find its own way out of its mess. Even Navvie. I wish she were rid of me and could go her own lonely way.

"If you're here for revenge, Whitey, if you're here to kill me as I killed you, then I will be very grateful."

I felt breath like hot brandy on my face and the white wolf licked both my eyes and the wound upon my face. It did not hurt at all, but shocked me like the kiss of Count Dinaos.

■ ■ ■

The king found me just before daylight, still sitting on the cold kitchen floor, sound asleep. "Are you in 'the belly of the wolf'?" he asked with heavy sarcasm. Climbing out of some dream I don't remember, I answered, "No. He didn't even bite." On my hands and knees I looked around the room, but there was no beast there.

"Did you let him out?"

King Benar sighed. "Too early for jokes, Nazhuret. I wanted to show you this"—and he handed me the Sekret padded jacket, which had been ripped up one side from waist to armpit. "I'm sorry I ruined your winter clothes, but upstairs you will surely find something that fits."

The house belonged to General Sir Hegl Skedar, who was a field commander for Gorham, and I felt no compunction about raiding his wardrobe, or his copper bath. It was not so easy, however, to find warm garb that was short enough for me without being sized for a lissome boy. Finally, I found a black wool shirt that could serve me as a long tunic, and a pair of boy's boots much softer and finer than my own. My ragged trousers had to remain in service. A servant volunteered the use of his sheepskin vest over all, and to this day I do not know whether that loyalty was for his master's sake or because he did not care particularly for his master.

Thus appareled, I looked like nothing Velonyan nor Rezhmian, but I did look warm. I went back to the kitchens and forced down some good breakfast I didn't want, sitting by myself in a corner, while King Benar breakfasted with the men who had hunted him the day before. When I was through, I stood behind the king in the position of servitor until he was compelled to notice me.

"So, Nazhuret," he said in a public voice, "you've given up on your brown tailored day wear. I do apologize." There was laughter.

I leaned forward and spoke to him alone. "You must give up something too, sir. If you would do what you came to do. You must send back this army."

His jaw made ridges along his face. "You must think me a fool, old man. I have camped around this house a good solid force of loyal soldiery."

I worked to retain my composure. "A good solid force of soldiery, whether loyal or disloyal, is not what a mediator needs most."

Benar looked around him, at the men at his table, where there was more gold on the uniforms than in the eggs and butter on the plates. "Perhaps this being a mediator is no longer necessary. I have found the men, the morale, the place, and the time . . ."

"You have found calamity," I whispered. I did not head for the frosted door into the kitchen, but into the halls, so it would be a while before the occupiers of the house figured my intent. I donned the sheepskin, my gloves, and left by the great door, into a blast of wind.

I circled to the back, where the stable court lay, and once within I considered appropriating one of the fresh horses, but Sabia, gaunt and tireless, stamped and whinnied. I saddled her and was out into the storm. My greatest regret was that I had not the time to inform Dinaos of the king's treachery—his treachery or my own, depending upon the views of the narrator.

Because of the blowing snow we could only walk, and there was no ring of sun in the sky to tell us in which direction to do so. I knew these parts fairly well, though, and turned the mare's head slightly to the right. Outbuildings formed and faded again, in the blinding snow. Sabia closed her ears against her head. My own ears were freezing.

Before us, on the public street, there was the pink of frozen blood and something dead. My poor mare found the energy to dance around it. I got off and saw white over white, outlined in red. It was impossible. It was the body of my white dog, my wolf, which I had killed a week before and which had licked me last night. I wondered who had seen the poor cringing creature and slain it, and I felt a strange regret, and then I saw without possibility of error that the wounds which had caused its death were those made by my own sword days ago, yet fresh and bloody. The body was warm.

What I did next was extravagant, considering my feelings and the press for time. I skinned the wolf, head, claws and all. I scraped the skin over the snow to remove most of the blood and then thought to throw it over the pillion of my saddle. I could not keep it there; it slipped one way and then another, and finally I almost lost it over the croup. On a bloody impulse I put the bloody thing around me, tying its feet around my neck and slipping the long snout over my bare head. The mare did not object, and indeed I had begun to think of her as a more ghastly animal than the wolf. White on white in white, we stepped through the blowing snow, and my only compass was the glow in the quarter of the sky that held the sun.

It was noon or later when I heard the shot, and my first impulse was to spin the mare and ride her back in her deep hoof-prints. But there had been something about that explosion, and then I had heard no whine of ball or impact in the snow or trees around me. I stood my nervous mare and waited, and up from the hill before me rose a figure covered by a sheet such as small boats use for sail. It was my little daughter and she was loading again. She waved when she knew I had seen her. I noticed that the pistol was a breechloader.

I trotted up to her. "So, you have perfected it." I said, and found to my surprise my lips were numb.

"I wouldn't call it perfect, Papa," she answered, busy fitting into the thing a brass cylinder that didn't want to go. "But it works more often than not. I had help in the foundrying." She pointed with her nose to a figure behind the trunk of a tree. Upon his head was a cap of snow, but even with this I could recognize the flaxen boy I had seen twice; once in the flesh. He looked as if he were not sure of his welcome.

"Are you a metalworker as well as . . . in the third order of the void, or whatever?" I asked him, and he answered, "Ironwork is my training, but I know something of brass. Your ball-casket is a good idea, because of the expansion of the metal. It seals . . ."

I told him I knew that already, and looked back at Navvie, who had loaded again and tucked the gun away. I noted with interest it was muzzle-down without losing the charge. "And do you have enough shells for your lead to waste one scaring your old father?"

"I don't have a loud voice," she answered.

Navvie, under her canvas wrap, was dressed after the manner of a boy of Vestinglon, in shirt, trousers, and tall stockings. Her disguise was not as perfect as those her mother had taken, but it served if a man did not look twice. I thought to tell her that a boy might be shot where a woman would escape, but she was old enough to know her own business, and besides, I was not sure I was right.

"And I was not certain you would recognize my voice, sir, and take it as that of a friend."

I looked down at the blond and ruddy fellow in his homespun and said, "I am good at remembering people who come to me glowing."

He looked embarrassed and with one hand divested himself of his snow cap. "So you got my message." His glance rose from my face to my own headgear. "May I ask why you killed your white wolf, sir?"

I thought how best to answer the question, and could think of nothing sensible. "I killed this wolf before you ever saw it by my side, lad." I was about to explain further, but he nodded solemnly and stepped back, leaving me to speak with my daughter.

"Your idea hasn't worked out, I'm sorry to say, my dear. I have been to the rebels and to the king, and all I have done is to instigate a winter campaign against the heights, led by the king himself."

Navvie was disappointed, but tried not to show it. "Then the worse for them, Papa. I guess I will have to end as the daughter of the king of Velonya."

"Horrid thought!"

She sniffed. "Do you think you could do worse than what is being done already?"

I shrugged, causing a rustle in the fur of the wolf. "I was speaking selfishly, Navvie."

The young man was staring over the ground whence I had come. His eyes were unfocused. I wondered if I ought to address him or let him meditate. Then he said, "There is a small party of horsemen following your tracks, sir. They will be in sight in a few minutes."

I didn't know what sense the boy was using to know this, but somehow I didn't doubt him. I cursed myself, feeling both fear for the young people and shame for my own sloppiness. "I depended on the blowing snow, children. I don't know how they tracked the mare, but forgive me."

"No need to suppose they're after you, Father, but in any case, let's withdraw a little. I doubt three men have a chance against us."

"The young are confident," I said, to no one but myself, but I followed Navvie to a place behind a little rise of ground. It would hide us, were we on our bellies, but not the standing horse. I had no idea what to do with her except slit her throat, and that seemed both ungrateful and noisy.

Navvie, however, was her mother's daughter. She soothed the beast with baby talk, and then gently she pulled one leg out from under her. The young man rubbed her with both hands on her muzzle under the eyes, and over she went, blinking but quiet. We joined the mare on the snow, and only the heels of the young people's snowshoes stuck up above the ground. Navvie spread the canvas over as much of us as she could.

First there was nothing to see over the long slope but blowing snow. My prints were already the merest pores in the young face of winter, and I began to doubt anyone could follow such a track. "What is she called: the mare?" asked Navvie.

I answered, "Sabia. Your mother had such another. Or per-haps the same horse. Things seem to be repeating in my life."

"Sabia! I was always told she was beautiful! And sweet."

I glanced at Navvie's ruddy cheeks, feeling slightly hurt by her judgment upon my horse. "This one could be beautiful, if I were not working her to death. And as for sweet—well, I never saw that in Sabia. But then, she was your mother's horse and I was nothing to her but occasional baggage."

"And this one is yours?"

I shrugged. "I seem to be killing this poor mare. Let's not talk about it. Just accept that she looks more like Arlin's Sabia than any creature I have yet met."

This talk about names reminded me of something. "Lad, lad. I am sorry to say I have never asked your name. Forgive my rudeness."

The blond gave me the grin of a child. "What are names, after all? What importance . . ."

"Enough! What is *your* name? The importance is that I have asked."

"My name is Timet, sir. Of no particular family. Born and raised in Norwess."

"Timet of Norwess," I said, and I laughed uproariously and rubbed my face with snow.

"Timet is a very common name, especially in Norwess," he said, but Navvie just looked from one of us to another with some of Arlin's dark intensity.

First the approaching party was a gray speck and then a wavering shape, like the leaf under water. Navvie passed me a small spyglass, but it fogged as I put my eye to it, and by the time I had cleared it, I could see the three riders with my fifty-five-year-old eyes, and if they were military trackers, I was a Harborman.

By the amount of gold in the gear of the leftmost rider I might have thought him the king of Velonya, but I recognized him as Dinaos and was very surprised. The neat uniform dress of the man to his right might have been that of the king's bodyguard, but I looked twice and saw the auburn hair of Benar himself. The third rider, slightly behind, was the mute pirate, Sieben. I watched them toil onward and marveled that they were entirely alone out here.

I inquired of Timet of Norwess for support. "Do your unusual senses tell you whether any accompany them, Tim?"

He blushed like a rose. "My senses are not that unusual, sir. But there is no one with the king but those two."

I pushed him further. "And why are they here? Can you tell me that?"

Navvie met my eyes, but she did not interrupt.

"Of course, to speak to Nazhuret of Sordaling. Why else?"

I was almost seduced by the boy's idea of my own importance. I myself could think of a few reasons the king would flee his own army: reasons not involving me. I did not let myself get into that argument, but I said, "So then, I'll go give them their wish."

"We'll cover you from here," he said, and damned if the boy didn't have a little bow made from a foil billet, just as Powl and I had carried thirty-five years before in our meanderings around the Sordaling suburbs. It looked to me like a charming but pathetic antique.

"We won't need to shoot," my daughter whispered to the boy. "Not while Count Dinaos is by."

"Who?"

I cut off their dialogue. "Don't shoot in any case, son. If Benar kills me and you kill him, then there is no one to rule in Velonya save the army, and that will mean the end of parliament and all my teacher and King Rudof cared for. And all I cared for, too."

I stepped over the snowdrift before he could respond, hearing only the crunch of my feet into the deep snow and the crackle of cold air in my nostrils.

I had called the boy "son" not casually, but because I was already fond of him, and saw in him a form of what I had been at his age, except that he was taller, more comely, and even odder than I was. I was also jealous of him, as though I might wish my tiny, beautiful Rezhmian mother to have been a strapping farm girl of Norwess. I was shamed by my own jealousy, but still I felt it. I floundered through the snow toward the horsemen, who struggled in my direction, and turned my mind back to the business at hand.

The king at least must have known me, for I had been wearing the black tunic and trousers on my last brief interview with him. The wolfskin rode down my back, so only part of my face was concealed from any man sitting above me. Still, they made no answer to my call, but wheeled and backed before deciding to stop and wait for me to stomp up to them. I saw their horses drop their heads and close their brown eyes against the ice in the wind. When

I came within a reasonable pistol shot, I flipped the head of the wolf off my hair, so that if I were shot it would not be out of mistaken identity.

Dinaos was the first to kick his horse closer. "By the heart of God, Nazhuret! What have you become now: a Sekret werewolf?"

I smiled up at him and felt the corners of my mouth crack. "My lord, compared with others I have met recently, I am as ordinary as a woolly sheep." I looked past him to the face of Benar, which the cold had turned white and red, like a Yule confection.

"I've . . . we've been chasing after you, Nazhuret," he said.

"Just the three of you?"

"Yes." The king seemed resentful, as though he expected gratitude for something, but my small vanity caused me to make the king's interests wait. "Did you track me?" I asked.

Dinaos answered, "No. There were no tracks. I didn't expect you would leave any, being who you are. But though I'm no wizard, neither am I stupid, and I guessed how you would choose the way up to Norwess. I do know you," he added complacently, and the king shot him a glance of distrust.

Behind me I heard Sabia scrabbling to her feet, her harness jingling. The king drove his horse closer to me. "Nazhuret," he said thickly, as numb-mouthed from cold as I was, "I must apologize. I let Gorman overpersuade me. That, and having all those soldiers under my own command unexpectedly. It was a sort of betrayal of you."

It was every sort of betrayal of me, but I saw no reason to tell Benar so when he was behaving so nicely. "I didn't intend this to be a maneuver in force, and indeed it will not be. I have sent . . ."

I glanced up into the wind and the king's face, but he was looking past me, his green eyes wide. "I have seen that man before!" He was pointing at my friend of the third level of the void.

"That's Timet of Norwess," I told them with some satisfaction.

Count Dinaos held his chin in one mittened hand and gave young Timet a heavy-lidded, judging stare.

"Fine-looking boy, isn't he?" I called to him, a shade sharper than I had intended. The count, unabashed, continued to stare.

"Bland," he announced at last. "But of course the young *are* bland."

I tapped the leg of King Benar to get his attention. "You say you sent the division home?"

"I did."

"And did it *go* where you sent it, sir?"

Benar tore his glance from the man he had seen walk right through him, shining like a mirror in the sun. He shook his head, not in reply to my question, but to clear his mind. I could see him already beginning to doubt Timet's original apparition. So do men eliminate from their past all miracles.

"Go home? I surely think so. With three rebellious generals and a field marshal in manacles. I am declared Commander of the Army, with authority to make peace, subject only to ratification from parliament. Parliament wants peace like a Cantoner wants a full ship. Now, Nazhuret, the rest of it is in your hands."

This made me laugh. I held up both hands, which were stuffed into mittens so thick they looked like the paws of a bear. "I hope not so, Benar, because my hands have lost all feeling."

■ ■ ■

There were six of us, four mounted and two on snowshoes. My daughter and Timet made much better progress than the rest. They seemed in unusually high spirits, given the situation, and I tried to say nothing that might mar that mood. We were approaching Norwess along the steepest road, which in small seemed to be only gentle elevation, dotted with trees and farmhouses and with every waterway bridged and covered, but when regarded in large was actually a ponderous switchback up the side of a mountain. We stopped at a cow byre for dinner, and though the place was bright in fresh paint and well maintained, it was empty. I had come with less in my bags than my companions, but with Sieben's provisions and Navvie's usual forethought I did not go hungry or dry. The horses ate what the cows were missing.

Benar wished to scout around the place for signs of what had happened, but Dinaos and I convinced him that Timet, being a local, could do it better. Navvie moved her kit over with the horses. She and the king had not gotten on since the day he called her a bastard to her face (and to mine). He had been eleven: far too old for a future king to engage in that kind of rudeness. If I remember correctly, it was because of this slip his father cracked him on the jaw so hard that he laid Benar out full length on his bedroom floor.

I stared covertly as he ate his cold dinner. Evidently his jaw had taken no permanent hurt. I wondered if I could ever like this king of Velonya. It would make things so much easier if I could.

I went out into the bright light and the wind to relieve myself. Since my training with Powl, I cannot piss on the dirt inside a building, even if the cows do. I saw Timet springing over the snow, swinging each leg out to spare the snowshoe. He stood close to me and bent his head to my ear. "We will meet the army at Norwess Palace, tomorrow before dark."

I stared around us. There was nothing in sight but a low fence and the snow-capped mound that was the cowman's cabin, abandoned and boarded over. "What here told you this, lad? No shadow of a track except yours and ours. I heard nothing."

Again he whispered, "Nothing told me. I knew it already. We retreated to the palace when this cold hit, and Navvie and I . . . your daughter Nahvah, I mean to say . . ."

"Say anything you like, Tim, but you should have said it to the king, whom it concerns most closely. Do you think I'm leading him into a trap?"

He shrugged. "I don't know what you are doing, Nazhuret. You never said."

I must be getting like Powl, I thought.

We went in and I told Benar that Timet's best guess was that we would find the army at the palace the next day. For a minute he did not say anything, but even in the dim light I saw his face grow taut and his eyes age. Then he said, offhandedly, "I wish we could make some extra miles today. It seems a shame to waste so much light."

I said I couldn't be sure of finding another shelter before nightfall. The king looked not at me but at Timet, who had remained standing in Benar's presence, though from respect or mistrust I could not tell. "Well, boy, *is* there another shelter?"

"No, sir," he replied. He stood attentively until certain that the king was finished with him, and then he faded back to the stall where Navvie had made her neat camp.

I guessed that Benar and Timet were nearly of an age, as Benar's father had been with me. For a few years Rudof had been in the habit of calling me "boy." I wondered how Timet felt about it.

That night I slept in front of one of the byre's two doors, hating the draft, while Timet guarded the other. I remember that Dinaos came over and prodded me to move so he could get out. When he returned to the byre, he sat down beside my bivouac.

For a while nothing was said, and then I thought it best to remind this reckless man that we were going into danger, and that his nationality and his connections were likely to prove unpopular. He replied smugly that he did not anticipate any danger. He was still sitting there when I closed my eyes, his lean profile lit by the snow-shine coming through a crack between doorboards. Just before I fell asleep it occurred to me that I still had not told Timet what I was doing with the king and an enemy count on the slopes of Norwess. How arrogant. How like Powl. No doubt his opinion of me would rise.

I did not sleep well because of the cold, and found myself shrinking unconsciously away from the door I had promised to guard. Sometime in the middle of the night I gave up and sat cross-legged on one of my blankets, wrapping the other over me, and spent the rest of the night in the belly of the wolf, the practice that seemed to be causing so much grief and misunderstanding to Velonya. I felt steeped in betrayal, though whether it was my betrayal of my country, my practice's betrayal of me, or any other passing betrayal I cannot tell. With the first light I was glad to be out. As I opened the byre door, a shaft of daylight slid over the floor, ending on the form of Timet of Norwess, who turned and opened his eyes. I left before I wakened the others.

I could see only one good end to this confrontation today, and that was like one fine thread in a tangle: hard to find, easily broken. If the king would not bend, it would likely end with all of us dead before nightfall. If the duke of Norwess would not accept rule of king and parliament, the same would occur. Perhaps Navvie and Timet might be spared from butchery, and Sieben considered no more than a servant, but no, Sieben would not likely abandon his master, nor would Navvie abandon her papa.

I worried more about my daughter that morning than I had when she was miles away and missing. I spoke my heart to Arlin about it.

"I like her with that boy," I said. "Perhaps it is desperation on my part, or self-love (because he carries my name), but if I could be assured that she had someone who meant something to her, I could go through with this political charade with much better heart."

I heard no answer in my head. I was trudging through cold and powdery snow, which reached half up to my knees and made little sparkling clouds in the still, dawn air. Ahead was a copse of second-growth osier, pollarded, with seats and a well in the middle. I saw the dark hair and a glimpse of the face, and wondered how Navvie had gotten past me in the dark. Doubtless she had left by Tim's door. I was glad I had not been near enough for her to hear me throwing her name and her future about out loud, and as I entered the copse, I tried to imagine who or what had been the Navvie-shaped lump in her blankets in the stall that the light had caught for me just that one instant as I was leaving the byre.

The head turned, and it was not Navvie but Arlin looking at me. All in black except her white face, and perfectly clear in the daylight. "It's enough, Zhurrie," she said. "I want you to stop talking to me now. I am dead. Let me be." And she was gone.

I thought I was going to weep loudly, but no sound came out. This was not self-control, but lack of strength. I stared with dry eyes at the sparkling surface of the bench, where the shade had left no imprint, and I choked repeatedly: blank inside, blank outside. I heard a shuffling sound behind me and someone dropped a blanket over my shoulders. I thought it was Navvie, but it was Timet. He moved in front and began to lower himself to the bench.

"Don't sit there," I said, but as he glanced from me to the snowy bench and back, I shook my head and swept the snow away for him. "I'm sorry, lad. Do sit down. What I said made no sense. It's the living who need the furniture, eh?"

He did sit. He had his own blanket wrapped around him, so that only the pale hair stuck out the top, floating and snapping in the dry air. "Who . . . do you want to tell me who it was, Nazhuret?"

"No. It doesn't matter anymore." As I spoke, it really didn't matter; I felt able to go on. I met the young man's eyes, glad at least that I had not screwed my face up in tears. A man of fifty-five crying is an unsettling sight. "Do you see them, Timet of Norwess? Ghosts?"

He winced. "Please don't call me that. It sounds too much like a title, and I'm common as dirt. But I have seen them, and spoken with them. It always hurts . . . I saw my father."

This was interesting. "So did I, once. My father, I mean. He looked like you."

Timet winced again. "Mine didn't. No matter. They are gone. We are here." He got up and strode off on his snowshoes with some dignity, and I was sorry I had ever teased the boy.

Most of the day four of us rode, while the ones with snowshoes padded on ahead and waited for us to catch up. My heart thudded with work and altitude. My frozen breath made breaking-glass sounds in my ears.

It was discovered that Count Dinaos and Timet shared boot sizes and before many minutes had passed, the count had convinced the young rebel to exchange the awkward baskets for his horse. It seemed odd, when Timet showed such a cold reserve before the Velonyan king, that he warmed so early to the aristocrat of Low-canton. But Dinaos, when he so chose, could exert an enormous charm.

Navvie was forced to spend the next hour shepherding Count Dinaos, and pulling him out of drifts. She giggled frequently, and so did the count. Timet, for his part, rode well and seemingly with enjoyment. He kept his stirrups short, Rezhmian style.

I let them play, for I felt this might be the last enjoyment any of us were to have, but I could not join in. I felt as empty and as cold as the sky, and even in the privacy of my mind I did not dare to speak. The king was as somber as I, and Sieben—well, the pirate did not appear to own a facial expression.

We passed tidy empty farms, and then we passed ones where the snow was churned with animal waste and human effort. The turns were sharp left and sharp right, one every few miles, and we did not stop. The snow receded to a covering no thicker than a feather quilt, and the road in many places was clear. The heavy, long-needled pines informed me when we were in that region anciently known as Norwess before Norwess was part of Velonya, or Velonya as such existed at all.

The king caught up with me. "I won't be able to talk," he said. "We will get there and at the important moment I will open my mouth and emit only frogs and toads."

"It's the altitude," I said. "I don't like it, either. You have to be born to it. Raised to it, I mean," I added, remembering that I had been born in the very house which was our destination.

A few minutes later, we passed a farm at the end of a long drive. I begged money from the king, trotted down, and came back balancing a heavy sack of corn over the pommel. Our spent horses were revived with good food and a half-hour's rest, and I gave the king the hide bottle I had bought from the farmer's wife. "For your throat," I said. "One sip now, and more when we near the palace."

He sprayed the brandy into his mouth and nearly gagged.

I told him it was good: that it contained herbs and honey as well as the refining of the grape. I explained myself so well he sprayed his throat again, heavily, and I had to wonder whether I should have kept the bottle.

Our own lunches were eaten side by side with those of our horses, and we were on our way just as the shadows started to grow again.

Timet had a very good power of estimation. We arrived upon the paved roads of Norwessten before the hour was up, and were in the town of white stone and white snow soon after. The young man led us, on his snowshoes once again, with my daughter scooting behind him. At my suggestion King Benar wrapped a blanket over his head. No sense, I told him, in exciting the townsfolk. Nor the many stalwarts holding their hands to the stove in the public houses or huddling in sixes and tens in the sunlight of the town square. Some of these looked dedicated and some looked like wild dogs, but I was learning to tell a rebel when I saw one.

Norwessten in snow was a dazzle to the eyes, but it is not a large town and we were soon through it. To go the three miles from the town to the palace needed no surveyman or tracker—we only followed the stream of men heading to and fro between them. Some of them were wearing the rebel "uniform," a white rag tied about the upper arm, while some were innocent even of that. Once we passed another beggar of Timet's sort, and they exchanged a signal with the hands that was half a salute. This was the first time I felt like laughing all day, but I restrained myself. The road was hard and dry.

The king knew that we were close also, for I heard him spraying his throat with brandy. He did not offer the bottle around, which was just as well.

I slipped off my poor mare and led her up next to Timet, who was carrying his snowshoes over his shoulder. "You have to get us in to see the duke," I whispered. "In private. Peacefully."

He furrowed his pink young forehead. "I don't have ready access to nobles, Nazhuret."

"Then you must baby-sit these here and allow me to do it, though I can't claim to be on any closer terms."

He glanced over his shoulder at king and company and recoiled. Like me, he had a speaking countenance. "No. I'll do it." He put the shoes under his arm and took off down the road at a run. For a moment I thought Navvie would follow him, but she remained with me.

We were in the parks of the palace and then we were on the avenue. "How are we doing, sir?" I called back to King Benar.

He answered with a few bars of the hymn "Velonyie," delivered in a strong tenor. I looked back in surprise, and the young king was smiling. "I'm not drunk, Nazhuret. Or not very. Now I need only decide what I'm going to sing to them."

Make it good, I said, but not very loudly.

As the park of Norwess Palace opened out into gardens, I began to see for the first time the rebellion's size. The snow was trampled so heavily that the grass locked below was clearly visible through the ice of compression, which was hard and slick every-where but on the road, where constant churning had warmed the stuff to a sticky mud. The place stank of what happens when twenty or forty thousand men are stalled together without proper latrines, and what had been in times past rose gardens, shrubberies, and plantings was now a city of shacks and tents. The air was gray with woodsmoke, and that of badly burned coal.

At my back the king said, "So this is the force that would overthrow the government?" He laughed, rather louder than I would have liked. "I wouldn't even call them soldiers. They can't keep their camps clean!"

I cleared my throat. "Be aware, sir, that there are twice the number of men here as you had when you wished to fling yourself at them the day before yesterday. And these are Norwessers, adapted to the altitude and to bitter cold. In fact, if they are camping in tents this month, they must be hardy as badgers. Let's keep your hood up and get through them quietly."

By now we were among the tents, where the stink was more of smoke than excrement. I was not happy over the change, however, for we had to squirm our way among the idle troops, mostly the hardy Norwessers I had just described, who moved out of the way of a man my size very reluctantly. Navvie, who by now must have been known among the rebels of Norwess, darted among them lightly, her own hood over her head, looking like any undersized boy of fourteen. King Benar had slipped down from his horse and was leading the animal along the "street" between the walls of canvas. I hoped he would not barge ahead of me.

Navvie led us down that street and another. At the end of the encampment was a rod of clear ground, much cut up by wagon wheels, and then the stairs of the second coach-portico of the palace. I felt Benar's hand on my shoulder and heard Dinaos's horse's hooves splash up beside us. The Lowcantoner count had not dismounted and rode with bare head, as though daring any one to challenge him for a foreigner. I could neither see nor hear Sieben, but I did not doubt he was nearby.

"Now what?" asked the king, and without looking at him, Navvie answered, "We wait for Timet to return. He will meet us here."

Now Dinaos got down, wincing, from his horse. "You know," he began, speaking Velonyie with more of an accent than usual, "I don't care for your northern saddles. Nothing more than wood and leather. They indicate to me that you don't expect to go very far when on horseback."

I glanced around, but there was no one at the portico but us to hear the count admitting his Lowcantoner birth. I saw the king looking also. He replied, "One day you will tease yourself into real trouble, Uncle. In fact, that day may be today."

I said to the count, "Velonyans pride themselves on their ability to withstand discomfort, my lord. In fact, though, their nether parts grow numb after a few miles."

The count eased himself down on the cold steps in his brocade smalls. "And you, Nazhuret? You have been riding on these saddles all your life. Are your nether . . ."

Hurriedly the king trod over the count's question with "If you feel our saddles are trying, Uncle, you should sit on one of the Rezhmian kind, with your knees up to . . ."

Navvie trod on *his* words with "He's here."

Timet was in the doorway, holding it open. I gave my horse to Sieben and went to him. I was stiff, too: a bad sign.

Timet did not look at us as we climbed up the marble steps and crossed to the door. Then all of us were within doors.

The warmth touched my face like loving kisses. There was baking in the air, and the smell of pickled cabbage. I felt a moment of such disgust for war, hardship, and politics that tears came to my eyes. I put my arm over my daughter's shoulder and gave her a brief hug.

"I told him you were back and had to see him quietly. The duke, that is. It was hard to get to him alone, but I did."

The king was staring across at Timet. "Oh, I imagine if anyone could get to a man alone, it is you, lad. In spirit, if not in body."

Timet stared back, so astonished that I wonder whether he had seen the king when the king had seen him. Then he led us down a curtained, carpeted hall and up a flight of stairs to a heavy black door, which he opened.

I had not understood the young man's arrangements. I intended to present the king to Mackim without the presence of my daughter, or Dinaos, or Timet, or anyone who might come in the way of lead or steel. But Timet stepped through the door with Navvie after him and the rest of us following at his heels. Inside was Duke Mackim of Forney, sitting at a heavy desk before a good fire, and, leaning against the same desk, the reedy figure of Jeram Pagg.

Jeram spoke first. "Excuse me, Nazhuret. I know you wanted privacy, but I have been longing to speak with you."

The duke was glaring at my party. "No matter, Pagg. It doesn't seem to be a very private meeting anyway."

I stepped in front of his scowling face. "I had hoped, my lord, for just the three of us." The king came up beside me and slipped his hood back.

There was a moment's silence, when it seemed events had the freedom to flow in any direction, like water. The king might bellow, or the duke call for his guards. But the duke might also go down on his knee to Benar: less likely, but possible. As it happened, Dinaos, his man, my daughter, Timet, the king, the duke, and myself all stood frozen, and it was Jeram Pagg who broke the possibilities into bits. He drew his dowhee.

"Put that down, Jer. There's no need for weapons here," said Nahvah, letting her heavy overcoat fall into a heap on the carpet.

Dinaos, who with his gentlemanly rapier was the only one of us to enter obviously armed, gazed full at Jeram's beggar garments and his hedger, at me, back again at Jeram, and began to laugh. It was a sturdier laugh than his lean person seemed to allow, and it drowned out King Benar's first words. "Call him off. I said call him off, Mackim. If I had come bent upon war I would surely make a better show of it than this."

Duke Mackim put his hand upon Jeram's arm and the dowhee came down, reluctantly. "I am very interested to know what it is you *have* come for . . ." I saw the duke floundering for a way to address Benar that would not admit the king's authority but would not be shockingly rude. There was no real difficulty, however, for we in Velonya have called our king by the title of any private gentleman for over fifty years now, and so Mackim called the king "sir." It is usual to give a little bow when "sir-ing" the king, but Mackim did not bow.

I was sure Benar missed none of these nuances, for they were his life's study and he was a sensitive man besides. But he did bow to the duke. "I have come alone—but for these few—in hope of mediating an end to this . . . fighting. This ruin of the countryside. This killing of Velonyan by Velonyan."

Mackim stared a long time at the king. He was rubbing his hands together as though cold. As he opened his mouth, there came a knock at the door, sharp and imperative. Somehow this sound was deeply alarming, and I imagined myself leaping the desk and duke together to reach Jeram's weapon and wield it. But the door was cracked open by Sieben, who put his silent face in the opening and wagged his index finger in an admonishing manner. His arrogant humility and servant's dress turned the trick; there was an apology, the door closed again and heavy steps receded.

"This talk of mediation sounds very odd coming from the man who is waging war against us."

"I am not!" Benar snapped a large palm on the polished walnut of the desk. "You know better than that! The army follows parliamentary majority, and if it were to follow one man it would be Lord Gorham or Marshal Pere, not a civilian of less than one year's experience of authority."

"He is right in that, my lord," I added as Mackim looked unconvinced. "Despite what you hear in Norwess, the king is not the instigator of this conflict. He has only been swept about by it."

Mackim sat back in his chair as the king leaned over the desk.

This was insufferable behavior, and even I, who have no manners, was shocked. "He may not be waging the war, but he is still the source of it." Mackim cleared his throat. "The truth of it is, the honest men of Norwess will not accept you as king, Benar. Not for any amount of threats or 'mediation.' "

Benar did not move. "Why? Do they think I'm not my father's son?" Mackim gave no reply to this, but played with a glove on the table. "Or do they think I killed my father?"

At this the duke glanced up sharply.

"Yes, I just recently heard that story—the man slandered is always last to know the gossip. Well, I will have you understand that I did not kill my father, nor do I know who did, if indeed he was killed and did not die naturally."

Mackim did not meet his eyes. "I never said you were guilty of that," he said, though of course all in the room knew he had said that. "But it is the connection. Lowcanton. We will not be ruled by a foreign country nor by foreign customs. Not in Norwess."

Foreign customs will sweep through this country west and east, up and down, as they always have, I said, but to myself. Just as our customs will travel wherever we happen to go. And Mackim's own dearest ways will change shape beyond recognition, yet he will not realize they have changed—not if he were to live a hundred years. Every day will be different, but man will see them all as the same.

All this I said to myself, with no hope that Mackim might understand. Nor the king. Nor anyone else.

Count Dinaos rustled politely at Mackim's mention of his homeland, and he gave a bland smile. Timet of Norwess, distrust in his honest face, stepped behind the desk and next to the duke, where he could keep an eye on the Lowcantoner. I saw Navvie's breechloading pistol in his sash, but he made no move to touch it.

"I don't intend to allow Velonya to be ruled by any foreign power, my lord duke. Even if I did, what would my desire mean to a nation with law legislated by three houses of parliament? If you use the person of the king as excuse for rebellion, you must be looking hard for an excuse."

Mackim glowered. "Now you are talking like your father. I thought your coronation meant a return to a strong monarchy."

The king sighed. "That language was no more than disguise for the creation of a strong military." His arms braced against the desktop, Benar hung his head, his auburn curls falling in his face. "I need your help in ending this war, Mackim."

Mackim folded his arms before him and looked past the king's belt buckle. "You admit you need my help, whereas I can end it without your interference at all . . . sir."

Now King Benar at last was getting angry. "Man, don't you care for the lives of your own soldiers? I am told they are piled like kindling by the roadside, waiting for the thaw to be buried."

Mackim's wince was barely perceptible. "Every man here is a volunteer. They are fighting for their own identity."

I said, "Shit!" I must have said it loud enough for all to hear, and strongly enough to get their attention. I took that opportunity to remove the coat I had stolen from Gorham, and the odor of the drying wolfskin that hung down my back rose unpleasantly. Its paws were tied beneath my neck and the nails clicked together as I tugged thoughtfully upon them. On impulse I hopped onto Mackim's desk.

"When a man starts to worry about his own identity he's lost it already. It's trying to board up the river to keep the water from flowing away. Soon you don't have a river anymore. When a nation starts to hug its own particularities to itself it is showing fear and it will soon cease having any characteristics worth saving. Velonya can't help being Velonya, and if the people are free and happy that's all one could want of it. Besides . . ."

I flipped the poor empty head forward until the nose overhung my face. ". . . Besides, Mackim, look what you have for alternative. Could anything be stranger, less comforting, more all-in-all foreign than myself?" As the duke glared, I displayed my barbaric suit, the bloody hide, and my own un-Velonyan face. "Note the touches of Sekret, of Rezhmia, of academia. Recall my sweet little mother, murdered by Velonyan hands when I was a babe. I don't forget her; believe me. And do mark my utter unpredictability—

remember how many men have called me mad over the years.
You've heard them.

"And now be aware that I am what you have as choice. Not
a Velonya ruled from Norwess, nor yet two snowy kingdoms at
the west of the continent, but Nazhuret, king of Velonya (and all
the Underworld, of course), at the head of a Rezhmian army of
occupation. The sanaur'l will supply the army. I will supply the
king."

I was prepared for a dangerous reaction from Mackim, or even
from King Benar, though he had heard all this before. What I had
not expected was to stare down the barrel of my own daughter's
experimental breechloading pistol, held by Timet of Norwess.

I should have told the boy what I was doing, after all.

"I can't believe I let you use me for this," he said, with a
shaking voice. The pistol did not waver in his hand.

"Don't, Tim. Let Papa be. You are acting out of ignorance,"
called Navvie, who was standing behind the king, in no position to
interfere.

"Ignorant, am I? Well, who kept me ignorant?" Timet's eyes
were almost soft; he was looking not just at me but at the whole
room of men. His stance was ready, almost relaxed. He seemed very
familiar with the firearm. I thought he was the most dangerous
opponent I had ever faced, except perhaps for Powl. I felt a draft
from behind, which crawled down my neck and told me I was
sweating.

I tried to equal his composure, though I was on the wrong end
of the gun for that. "What *did* you think I was coming here for, lad?
How can I end a war in which each side is willing to destroy its own
people, except with a threat even worse?"

"What you offer is certainly worse, Nazhuret. You tell no lie
about that. Though I have studied the arts and sciences of Rezhmia
for years, I will not endure to have that country ruling my own.
That you could think of it . . ."

Looking at this large, blond, long-boned young man behind
the pistol, I found myself starting to smile. "Well, you see, Tim—
you're a Velonyan. I'm a half-breed. For me it's different."

"But in all your writings you always claimed to be . . ."

I cut him off before he could finish. "I have published no writings. Perhaps the philosophy you think mine belongs more properly to Jeram Pagg, here."

Jeram pounded the desk. "You lie, Nazhuret. I added nothing. Nothing!"

I was chilled in the breeze from the door, but refused to allow a shiver to start, because fear would turn easily to terror. I heard the men around me shifting, and the hiss of Count Dinaos's rapier along the scabbard. I wondered on whose behalf he was drawing it. Mackim looked behind us and then away. Jeram looked behind us and then carefully at me, a message in his eyes. Timet squeezed the trigger.

The slug stung my ear and deafened me. For a moment I was back in time, when I was twenty-three and exploded in a petard set off by Rudof's men. I was not able to hear the lead slam into the body of the man who had come into the room as I spoke, and who had pointed his own, less modern pistol at my back, and been slain by Timet of Norwess.

"Foul, my lord duke!" shouted the king. "Unworthy and stupid!" He backed against the wall, seemingly shocked by the nearness of the shot and the stink of powder.

After the first stagger, I did not move. "Mackim, you *are* a fool. Did you think killing me would dissolve the danger? You have the choice of Rezhmia with me or Rezhmia without me—a much less inviting plan, believe me—or of making my . . . I mean, *this* country single again. It is our weakness that forces the sanaur'l's hand. They cannot afford a Velonya in service to Lowcanton. Neither will they accept a coup from Norwess, or the army."

"How do you know this: that the Rezhmians won't accept a change in monarchy?" asked Mackim, who had not moved from his chair. "One Velonyan ought to be as good as another to a country that is perennially feeding ground glass to its own nobles."

I had to sigh. "My lord, you don't understand the Rezhmians any better than the average Velonyan does, and that is very badly.

Besides, the only Rezhmian nobles fed ground glass in the last fifty years or so were my mother and uncle, who were not poisoned by Rezhmians but by a Velonyan duke who once sat in the same chair you now occupy. Believe me, Mackim, they will take the present king—with a curb on Lowcanton influence—or myself, or a protectorate of their own. You have your choice.

"That's all. I've said what I came for." I stepped toward the door and Mackim called to me, "And you don't even wait for an answer?"

"No. I'm through as messenger boy. Besides—my horse is tired."

As I strode out, I brushed by the king of Velonya. On impulse, I looked at him and added, "You have your choice, too. You can come with us. For your safety."

"My safety?" The king wore a predatory but not angry smile. "Nazhuret, you are the least safe companion I have ever known. I shall stay and mediate, as I said I would.

"I may even enjoy it," he added under his voice. Perhaps he still felt the brandy.

I did not know if I would live past the moment I crossed that threshold. Mackim shouted after me, "We have men enough to stand against Vestinglon *and* Rezhmia!"

I did not pause, but I heard Timet's quiet, young voice. "My lord duke," he said. "You haven't as many men as you think. You have lost your banner. You have lost your wolves," and he strode behind me. Ahead came Dinaos and his man, and the count shouldered me between them. Beside me stepped Nahvah, once more in possession of her experimental pistol. I bent to her ear. "It works," I said. "Very nicely, eh?"

She shrugged. "So far."

We passed through the door and past a clutter of uncertain guards in the finery of the duke's personal service. Lacking orders, they did nothing. Sieben ran ahead, and by the time we came into the daylight, he had the horses. We mounted, watched by a dozen whispering men. As I watched out of the corner of my eye, Jeram Pagg squeezed out the door and ran to us. He stood below my gray mare and stared up at me, wordlessly, and then he walked to where Timet was lacing his snowshoes. I saw the young man shake his head, but did not hear the question. We came out from the camp almost as quietly as we came in, leaving only the king behind.

"Don't you want to stay with your nephew?" I asked Dinaos. "He may need some assistance, and as I am the threat which is to bind Velonya together, it is not appropriate that I give it."

Dinaos's face was as ironical as Powl's in his worst moments. "But I am the equal and opposite balancing threat, being from Lowcanton. Therefore it is also appropriate that I leave. And then, I do not like my nephew, O barbarian. I did not come all this way to baby-sit my nephew. Now that this dreary ride is over, it is for us to go somewhere more interesting. It is the time I spoke to you about, once before. Perhaps better than the first meeting. Perhaps worse. But different. I swear to you—different."

My ears were blushing. I knew this because the injured one was stinging like mad. "But I don't know where I'm going, Count. And . . . I don't know . . . I don't know . . ."

He grinned and his eyes glittered in the snow-light. "I know that you don't know, barbarian. You don't know a thing. So what?"

We had entered the park by now. Timet, skimming over the snow at the side of the icy road, leaned over to me. "Would you have done it, Nazhuret? Would you have come in with an invading army? Or was it an act to make those fools get together? I need to know—would you have done it?"

I was glad for any interruption: even this one. "Those fools? You mean the king and the duke? You have as little manners as I do, Tim. And my answer is that I would not like to do it. I hate war and I would hate being monarch, both for my country's sake and for my own. But I would have done it. I still may."

He stopped abruptly, raising a little cloud of snow. "You said in there that it wasn't your country."

I didn't bother to answer that one.

Not ten minutes later, Navvie bounced up on her snowshoes

with a great deal of determination in each stride. "Papa," she called to me. "You don't need me anymore. Not with you all the time." I said nothing and she went on. "It used to be you were so lonely I couldn't bear to part. Then, I think my being with you kept you lonely. I don't know any other way to say it but that. So I'm going away."

"It's a good time for it," I admitted.

"With Timet."

"I guessed that part of it," I added, and tried not to grin. Then I noticed my daughter was in tears. I slipped off the horse and held her awkwardly, hampered by the huge snowshoes. "Why be sad, Navvie? Nothing is lost. Nothing."

Timet was standing behind her, carefully not intruding. "That's easy to say," she sobbed, and she embraced me so fiercely I could not speak. Then she turned her snowshoes, spraying white powder, and ran lightly over to Timet.

"It's not," I called after her. "Not really easy to say. It takes all my effort."

I got back onto my beautiful, bony horse and looked over at Dinaos, who was waiting patiently, all expression veiled. "So, barbarian?" he asked, and then he smiled. "What happens now?"

I watched the sunlight sparkle on the snow, laced with shadows. I wondered where Sieben had gotten to, and the troublesome Jeram Pagg. For the first time in years, I felt no anger toward the fellow.

I said, "I have no idea what happens now."

■ ■ ■

My father lived almost ten years after these events, and a number of portraits of him exist, all by Dinaos. Ironically, one is on display in the Royal Gallery of Lowcanton. After this narrative, however, it seems he wrote no more.

My father begged me repeatedly that any manuscripts of his that might fall into my hands I would burn, to save trouble for all involved. Each time, I assured him I would do no such thing. Yet, I find I have been declared the executrix of his estate. (It is a small estate.) In this I perceive Papa's ambivalence toward his own compositions. Or his idiosyncratic sense of humor.

Since the day I left my father in the woods, I have never heard the voice of my dead mother. Though she was a good mother to me, she was always his companion first. Nor have I heard or seen my father since his death.

But then, I am not lonely.

N.H.